BENEATH

BENI

EATH

ROLAND SMITH

Text copyright © 2015 by Roland Smith
www.rolandsmith.com

Library of Congress Cataloging-in-Publication Data

Smith, Roland, 1951– author.
Beneath / Roland Smith. — First edition.
     pages cm
Summary: Pat O'Toole has always idolized his older brother, Coop, right
up until the day Coop ran away from their home just outside Washington,
D.C. — now a year later he has received a package containing a digital voice
recorder and a cryptic message from his brother, which will lead Pat on a
strange and dangerous journey to the mysterious Community living beneath
the streets of New York.
ISBN 978-0-545-56486-1
1. Brothers — Juvenile fiction. 2. Cults — United States — Juvenile fiction.
3. Radicalism — United States — Juvenile fiction. 4. Attempted murder —
Juvenile fiction. 5. New York (N.Y.) — Juvenile fiction. 6. Washington
(D.C.) — Juvenile fiction. [1. Brothers — Fiction. 2. Underground areas —
Fiction. 3. Cults — Fiction. 4. New York (N.Y.) — Fiction. 5. Washington
(D.C.) — Fiction.] I. Title.
PZ7.S65766Be 2015
813.54 — dc23

                                                    2014018647

10 9 8 7 6 5 4 3 2 1   15 16 17 18 19

Printed in the U.S.A.   23
First edition, February 2015

The text type was set in Garamond.
The display type was set in Impact.
Book design by Phil Falco

For my wife, Marie, who has always
wanted me to write a Christmas story,
although I realize that this may not be
the story she had in mind

DOWN THE RABBIT HOLE

Exactly one year to the day after my brother, Coop, ditched me, I got a package in the mail.

It came to the school, not our house.

The secretary handed me the package with a warning that I was never to use the school as my personal address.

I was going to tell her that I hadn't when I saw my name: Pat Meatloaf O'Toole, scrawled in Coop's familiar handwriting.

Meatloaf is not my real middle name.

I told her I would never do it again, grabbed the package, locked myself in a restroom stall, and tore the box open.

Inside was a handheld digital voice recorder, a supply of memory sticks, and a note written on a greasy hamburger wrapper:

Lil Bro, Pat, just turn the recorder to Play
and I'll explain what you're supposed to do with
this. DO NOT share with parents. This is just
between you and me.
Your Big Bro, Coop

I made sure the restroom was empty and switched on the recorder.

Hey, Meatloaf, I know you're mad at me for splitting without so much as a good-bye, or a note, but opportunity knocked. I'm not sure what Mom and Dad told you, but while you were at school we had one of our discussions about my future. As usual, it was one-sided — a monologue, not a dialogue — and their plans for me did not include anything I was interested in doing . . . big surprise. So I packed my things and walked out the door while it was still open.

I would have called and explained, but you know my take on the whole phone thing. Then I was going to write you a letter, but the longer I waited the longer the letter got in my head. Pretty soon it was too long to write. Know what I mean? So I bought a second digital voice recorder exactly like the one I've been using in my travels and figured you and I could stay in touch on the little memory sticks that store the recordings.

And the truth is that I want to hear your voice, and I hope that you still want to hear mine. So consider this a slow-motion cell phone.

You'll be able to transcribe all this into one of those jour-nals you're always scribbling in.

Epistolary. Remember that?

Now, memorize this address: PO Box 1611, New York, New York. Zip: 10011. This is where you can send the mem-ory sticks when you figure out how to use the recorder. And it would be nice if you would respond soon so I know you got the recorder and that you're okay. Here's another address you need to know: PO Box 912 at the post office on Elm Street. That's your private mailing address in McLean. You pass the post office every day on your way to and from school, so it shouldn't be a problem for you to pop in and check the mail. The PO box key is buried in the pot with the petunias Miss Flower planted in the backyard. I assume that Mom and Dad still haven't hired anyone to do any landscaping since the Flowers were fired. And I'm certain you haven't done any yard work, so the key should be there. Talk to you soon, Lil Bro.

Only Coop would think of something like this. That's how his mind works. But the recorder was a huge technological leap for him. I think this is the first electronic gadget he has ever owned.

The little recorder has a lot of functions. There's software with it too. I can edit the recordings, splice them together — like I'm doing now — then transcribe them in my journal.

A hybrid journal.

A collaboration with my brother.

The thumb switch on the side has five positions:

Play.

Fast-forward.

Rewind.

Record.

Erase.

Down the rabbit hole we go.

ONE

UP TOP

A LITTLE FAMILY HISTORY

...for my eyes...I mean, for my ears *only...in order to practice with this recorder.*

I don't think I'll send this to Coop, but I might change my mind if I don't sound too stupid.

My brother, John Cooper O'Toole, is five years older than me. And I'm not embarrassed to say that I have idolized Coop my entire life, from the day my baby blue eyes understood that the boy with curly brown hair, green eyes, and the idiotic grin always leaning over me was my brother.

I'm definitely not sending this to Coop...

Rewind...

I can get rid of the last words or...

Fast-forward...

Insert...

(I can insert things I forgot or want to clarify.)

Or I can keep it even though it sounds stupid, which I think I'll do...

Record...

Coop was not the child my parents expected.

I wasn't either.

But you don't get to pick your parents, and they don't get to pick you.

My parents *did* pick each other before Coop came along though, which is one of the unsolved mysteries of the universe.

Mom is an astrophysicist and former astronaut.

Dad is a molecular biologist and Nobel laureate.

Mom is always looking up. Dad is always looking down.

Neither of them looked at us much.

Mom wanted girls.

Dad didn't want kids at all.

Here's how Coop put it: With their combined DNA they expected filet mignon. When they opened the oven they got two pans of meatloaf.

Within months of Coop's abrupt departure, by mutual consent, my parents split up.

Mom is dating an old man with three young daughters.

Dad is dating a young woman with an old parrot.

WE ALL HAVE LITTLE QUIRKS

but Coop has more than most.

I think it's because he was born during a lunar eclipse.

December 24.

Christmas Eve.

Two weeks before he was supposed to pop out.

Dad raced Mom to the hospital and got snagged by the worst traffic jam on the 495 Beltway in Virginia history.

People simply stopped their cars in the middle of the highway to watch the sky.

Mom was furious.

But not at the motorists who decided to turn the highway into a parking lot.

It was the timing.

She wanted to see the eclipse just as badly as those who were blocking her.

Instead, she was lying on the backseat of their brand-new SUV in agony, trying to squeeze out her first child.

A boy.

Coop has a different take on his quirks.

Prior to his birth, Mom went on two space shuttle missions.

Coop believed that during the second mission . . . *something happened*. (He always whispered those last two words.) What *happened* was never explained.

From the day Coop was born he rarely slept at night.

The pediatrician assured my parents that Coop would outgrow this behavior.

The doctor was wrong.

Mom and Dad both worked, so they hired a full-time nanny to take care of him at night. And a second full-time nanny to watch him sleep during the day.

The nannies were sisters.

Identical twins.

Spinsters.

Camilla and Cecelia Flores, who didn't speak ten words of English between them. We called both of them Miss Flower because their last name was the Spanish word for *flowers*.

We suspected they switched shifts, covering for each other when necessary, sometimes working twenty-four hours in a row. It didn't matter to us because we couldn't tell them apart anyway — they were identical down to the moles on their upper right lips with three black hairs growing out of them. They were the same person split in two.

The Flowers taught Coop to flamenco dance when he was three years old.

By the time I came along he had switched to tap and never looked back.

Coop and I used to watch YouTube clips of the great tappers like the Nicholas Brothers, Leonard Reed, Honi Coles, Bojangles, Fred Astaire . . . Coop was as good if not better than all of them. He sometimes tapped for me and the

Flowers, but mostly he tapped by himself for himself. Several nights a week he'd drape his tap shoes around his neck, sneak out of the house, find a tunnel or highway underpass, and tap until dawn.

I asked him one time why he tapped.

"To keep my feet moving, Lil Bro," he answered. "You're not going anywhere if you don't keep 'em moving."

When I was nine and Coop was fourteen, Mom and Dad let the Flowers go. It was like losing two mothers at the same time. And it turned out to be a big mistake, because it left Coop and me on our own. But I'll get to that later.

Back to Coop's quirks . . .

He collects flashlights. (Hundreds of them from all over the world.)

He loves people but doesn't crave their company, sometimes staying in the house for weeks at a time. (I guess I better explain: Old people, young people, rich people, poor people, white, black, Hispanic, Muslim, Christian, whatever . . . he makes no distinctions. To him they are just people . . . none better, none worse than the other. I think people sense this in Coop, because they are attracted to him like moths are attracted to light. I don't know why this is. Something in the way he moves? Pheromones? I've seen complete strangers cross a busy street to talk to him. But the conversations are a little one-sided. Coop will nod, shake his head, frown, smile, and say only enough to keep them talking. When they walk away Coop knows all about them, but they know virtually nothing about Coop.)

He has never worn a watch. (A minute, hour, day, or month are all the same to him.)

He has never sent or received an email.

He does not know how to drive a car.

He writes short letters to people he doesn't know on purple stationery in beautiful script and doesn't include a return address.

He does not talk on the phone. (Ever.)

He slept virtually all the way through school (and was late every day) but graduated with honors because he did his homework — at night — and turned in all of his assignments on time.

He was accepted to every university my parents filled out the applications to. He rejected all of them.

He has no close friends, yet everyone is his friend.

I thought that I was his best friend until he took off without telling me. I know that sounds whiny, but it hurt. I was really ticked off at him. It was worse than losing the Flowers. I was tempted to send a recording back consisting of just two words with an exclamation point. But that idea lasted about two seconds. I was too happy to hear from him to stay mad.

HERE ARE SOME OF COOP'S
FAVORITE THINGS

Favorite activity: Three-way toss-up . . . tapping, reading, writing.

Favorite book: Another toss-up . . . *Dracula* by Bram Stoker, written in 1897, and *A Journey to the Center of the Earth*, written by Jules Verne in 1864.

He must have read both of these books a dozen times. And he read them to me when I was eight, giving me nightmares for months. Especially *Dracula*. Coop assured me that there were no such things as vampires. He said that the reason the novel had so much effect on me was because Stoker had chosen to write it in a style so realistic the story appeared to be fact. The technique is called epistolary, from the Latin *epistola*, meaning letter. The author uses fictitious diaries, letters, and newspaper articles to tell the story. But the nightmares continued, and bats still creep me out. What does an eight-year-old know, or care, about epistolary novels?

Just think what Stoker could have done with a digital voice recorder and email.

This is what I'm doing here in this journal . . . stringing together bits and pieces of information to make a story, each bead in the necklace made from different material.

Memory beads. Recorded beads. Newspaper beads. Letter beads . . .

Coop got me hooked on keeping a journal. He gave me my first one and said I should keep a diary and never let anyone read it, including him. He said showing someone your diary was like offering someone a slice of your soul. "Too many slices, Meatloaf, and pretty soon the plate is empty. No soul food left, Lil Bro."

Which reminds me . . .

Favorite food: Tuna fish sandwiches.

Favorite drink: Water.

Favorite quote: "Listen to them, the children of the night. What music they make!" (Count Dracula to Jonathan Harker when the wolves howl outside the castle on Jonathan's first night there.)

Favorite music: Anything with drums.

Favorite smell: Freshly turned dirt.

Which brings me to . . .

THE GREAT TUNNEL DISASTER

as it became known, started the day after the Flowers were dismissed. (Or *weeded*, as Coop put it.)

I'm not talking about a little hole in the ground or a small cave. I'm talking about a real full-blown tunnel that any mining engineer would have been proud of. Coop must have been planning it for months, or even years. He had drawn up elaborate schematics and complicated mathematical equations. He had collected shovels, sledgehammers, picks, wheelbarrows, wooden posts for beams, planks for the walls and ceiling, scuba gear in case he ran out of air . . . all stored in the shed in back of the house, which neither of my parents ever went into.

I was recruited as his assistant engineer and coconspirator after I swore on his favorite possession (his tap shoes) that I would not tell a living soul about his plan. It was easy to keep that promise because there really wasn't a plan. Plans have endings. Coop's tunnel only had a beginning hidden behind the shed.

Mom and Dad thought Coop was lazy and lacked drive. I guess they never took into account the time it took him to dig the tunnel, which authorities later determined was more than a mile long.

Coop was inside that muddy tube every single night, week

after week, for eight months. When he hit an obstacle he couldn't break through he would go around it, over it, under it — the tunnel slithering beneath the neighborhood like a giant earthworm.

His nightly routine was to wake up around eleven, eat a tuna fish sandwich, then walk across the backyard to the shed, where he would change into his digging clothes — my mom's yellow rain slicker and pants. It was cold in the tunnel and wet. When he finished digging for the night he'd rinse off the mud with a garden hose, dry himself with an old towel, change into his jeans and T-shirt, and sneak back into the house.

On school days I was Coop's alarm clock. My job was to get him out of the tunnel before my parents woke up. On weekends I joined him in the tunnel. My job was hauling buckets of dirt and dumping them into the wheelbarrow.

About four months into the project Coop broke through a wall of dirt and discovered a cavern.

"I knew it!" he shouted. "I knew there was something down here."

What he had discovered was his own tunnel from a month earlier, evidenced by the molding tuna sandwich inside the Ziploc bag lying on the tunnel floor. Somehow he had gone in a complete circle and bumped into his old lunch.

Coop kept digging.

The longer the tunnel became, the slower the progress. Every scoop of dirt had to be wheelbarrowed back to the entrance and dumped into the stream that ran down the gully in back of our house. He started punching head-size holes in the surface every few nights to figure out where he was, hoping to find a closer dumping site.

One night a dog bit him on the nose.

Coop still kept digging.

A flashlight was fine for finding his way down the dark tunnel, but for digging he used a lantern. The fuel lasted a hundred times longer than batteries and was cheaper.

Coop found a second dump site about a quarter mile downstream from the shed and was once again making good progress on the tunnel. He had also discovered some artifacts: a handful of musket balls and a rusty bayonet he claimed were from the Civil War.

Spring break was a few weeks away, and a couple of months after that, school would be out.

"We'll have the whole summer to dig," he said. "Who knows what else we'll find!"

On the last night of the project we found a gas line.

It was a Saturday morning a little after three.

The night before, Coop had bumped into the Mesas' Olympic-size swimming pool and was digging along the side of it, hoping he had chosen the shortest way around. He was grunting so loudly in the confined space while he swung the pick he didn't hear the hissing noise.

I was lying right behind him waiting for the next bucket of dirt.

"Do you hear that?" I asked.

"What?" Coop said, taking another swing with the pick.

16

"Do you smell that?"

"I don't smell anything except my own sweat. The pool is heated, and the wall is warm." He moved the lantern to a better position. "I can hardly wait until we get around this thing. I can't believe I bumped into it. Of all the luck. At least we won't have to shore up this side of the —"

Coop swore, then yelled, "Run!"

The tunnel was not tall enough to run in. I crawled on my hands and knees as fast as I could, with Coop's head bumping into my rear. We were twenty yards from the second entrance when we heard the *wumpf!*

I didn't see the fireball because Coop had straddled my back and covered my head with his body. The last thing I remember was feeling as if I was flying down a muddy rifle barrel like a musket ball with Coop hanging on to me.

I woke up in the hospital three days later. Mom was sitting next to my bed reading an article in the *Journal of Astrophysics* called "The Formation of Polar Disk Galaxies."

"How's Coop?" I asked.

"He is insane," Mom answered.

Except for some burns and singed hair, Coop was fine.

The same could not be said for our neighborhood.

McLean is across the Potomac River from Washington, DC. Aside from former astronauts and Nobel laureates we have senators, CIA agents, Georgetown University professors, lobbyists, and other people, like the vice president's daughter and her family, whose house is kitty-corner to ours.

Two hundred local, state, and federal law enforcement agents arrived within minutes of the explosion. They thought it was a terrorist attack.

It didn't take them long to figure out that it was only Coop. Every inch of his tunnel had collapsed, which led them directly to the shed in our backyard.

I missed everything after the fireball, but I heard about it after I came out of my coma.

The blast blew us right past the second entrance. Coop and I caught on fire, or at least our pants did, but we were put out by the water from the Mesas' swimming pool. Mostly.

Through all of it Coop hung on to me.

He dug us out of the collapsed tunnel with his bare, blistered hands, stopping every few seconds to blow air into my lungs.

He carried me across our back lawn to my waiting parents and several federal agents, looking like the Creature from the Black Lagoon. Our pants were still smoking.

Dad took me.

The Federal Bureau of Investigation took Coop. They hustled him into the back of a black sedan and drove him away before anyone in the neighborhood saw him.

The whole thing was hushed up. The headline the next morning read: "Gas Line Explosion Scares McLean." I think our family was the only one who knew what really happened.

By the time I got out of the hospital, a couple of days after I regained consciousness, you wouldn't have known anything bad had happened in the neighborhood. The lawns had been repaired, the flowers replanted, and the five trees that were knocked down were cut up and hauled away. The only thing still being worked on was the Mesas' pool. (They ended up having to replace it.)

Two FBI agents came by the house. An Agent Ryan did all the talking. She told us that in the interest of national security they were going to stick with the gas-line-explosion story. She said that people were already jumpy enough with all the terrorist threats. It wouldn't do anyone any good to know that a fourteen-year-old dug a mile-long tunnel and blew up a swath of one of the most secure neighborhoods in America.

(I'm probably violating some state secrets act by writing about it here.)

They let Coop go a few days after I got home.

His hands were wrapped in bandages.

He said they kept him in a nice room with a comfortable bed and brought him a tuna sandwich whenever he asked for one. Several times a day different people came into the room asking the same questions over and over again. But mostly he talked with Agent Ryan, whom he got along with well.

There wasn't much my parents could do to punish him.

They couldn't ground someone who doesn't care if he can't leave the house.

They couldn't take away the phone, computer, or TV from someone who doesn't use any of them.

They could have taken away his tap shoes, but they knew he would just tap in regular shoes or his bare feet — muted tapping.

"No more tunnel digging," Dad said.

Coop agreed.

Later, up in his bedroom, I asked him about his hands.

"No big deal. I got some blisters when I put out your pants. They got infected when I dug us out." He hesitated and tears came to his eyes. "The worst part of it was thinking that I killed you, Meatloaf."

Coop would have gotten out of the tunnel a lot faster without having to drag me through the suffocating muck.

Coop hung on to me with blistered hands.

Coop filled my lungs with air from his lungs.

Coop could have died trying to save me.

More than the tunnel had collapsed that terrible night.

After that, things weren't the same between Coop and me.

We were brothers.

We were friends.

But he no longer confided in me. It was as if we were in separate passageways.

When Coop talked to me, there was an echo now.

I couldn't tell where he was.

When I complained about it he said, "I've got to travel my path, and you have to travel yours."

THE DAY COOP LEFT

I searched his room to see what he had taken with him.

Tap shoes. (Which were the only Christmas gift he had ever accepted from anyone. I got them for him last Christmas because the pair he was using looked and smelled like road-killed opossums.)

Half a dozen flashlights.

Some clothes.

A two-man tent.

A sleeping bag.

A beat-up backpack.

He left behind his purple stationery and envelopes.

Coop's life did not revolve around things.

HI, COOP

Sorry it took me so long to send this recording, but I didn't want to sound like an idiot, so I had to practice for a while. I would have rather written you a letter, but you said you wanted to hear my voice. So here it is . . .

Mom and Dad have separated.

Mom has a boyfriend. Dad has a girlfriend.

If it works out, you will have three half sisters, a stepfather, a stepmother, and a half parrot.

Mom is with a widower named Wayne, a real estate lawyer in Boca Raton, who has three daughters under the age of five. She moved to Florida. Dad is with a girl not that much older than you. Just kidding. But she is a lot younger than Dad. Her name is Denise. She's an ornithologist. She and Dad go birding almost every weekend, leaving me home alone with the parrot. I guess this is good, because Dad's looking up now instead of down . . . at least on the weekends.

I was ballistic when you took off without telling me, and mad for months when you didn't contact me.

I'm over it now. I guess.

What are you doing? Where are you working? What's it like there? Where do you live? How long are you going to stay wherever you are? Are you tapping? Are you ever coming back here?

▶

Holy cow, Pat. A half parrot? I always wanted a parrot. I guess half a parrot is better than none. But I'm sorry to hear Mom and Dad split up. They may not have been pleased with the two meatloafs they baked, but they seemed happy with each other . . . at least most of the time. I hope they get back together . . .

Me?

I've been exploring. I know that New York City is only a few hours by train from McLean, but I took the long way around, hitching to California, up the West Coast through Oregon and Washington, then back east across Canada, dropping down from Quebec.

When I finally got here I knew I was in the right place. What I'm looking for is here. I don't know how to explain it, but I can feel it . . . It's close.

I know you're wondering: What is Coop looking for? You're not alone. So am I. All I know is that something has been pulling me my whole life like some kind of cosmic magnet, and I think the magnet is buried someplace here. I need to find it and ask it what it wants.

I'm not working. I'm not looking for work. I live wherever I am at the end of the night. I'll stay here until I find whatever it is I'm looking for. In the meantime there's a lot to see. I have a lot to learn. And of course I'm still tapping. The shoes you gave me are magical.

I'm running a little low on batteries. I think there's still some up in my room. Throw them in with the next recording. I'll cut this short because I need to find a stamp and an envelope and catch the postman. Wonderful to hear your voice, Meatloaf. I mean that. I miss you. Everything is good here . . .

Coop, I found the batteries in your room along with your purple stationery. I've included some of it with some stamps. Not much to talk about here. School. Homework. Neighborhood. On weekends it's just me and the parrot most of the time. His name is Vincent and he doesn't like anyone except Denise, who's had him since she was a little girl. He's chewed up some things around the house and screams a lot, but Dad doesn't seem to care. He's changed since he and Denise got together. Smiles more. He's exercising. He bought an expensive pair of binoculars. A couple of days ago I came home from school and he was wearing jeans, an untucked polo shirt, and Birkenstocks. He's growing his hair out. He doesn't shave on weekends. At night he and Denise spend a lot of time looking at topographical maps and bird guides. They listen to recorded bird calls and test each other. Denise wins every time.

Hey, Lil Bro . . . I'm at the library today getting out of the rain, doing some research. I met this old guy who knows everything about New York City . . . especially underground. He turned me on to a bunch of books about it.

Here are some interesting New York City factoids . . .

For the first two hundred years pigs were used to clean the streets. Twenty thousand of them!

The city is built on rock, but there are hundreds of streams, springs, and sucking sand-whirls beneath New York. In fact, the New York Public Library, where I'm sitting right now, is on top of the Murray Hill Reservoir, where the city used to get its water.

There are one hundred and seventy varieties of precious and semiprecious stones in the rocks beneath the city. Amethysts, opals, beryl, tourmalines, garnets . . . Whoa! Hang on . . .

I just hopped a subway uptown . . .

I'm at the American Museum of Natural History now looking at one of the biggest garnet crystals ever found in the US. It came out of a ditch on West Thirty-Fifth Street. Before they put it on display here someone was using it as a doorstop.

In this one I thought I'd just take you through one of my nights here in the city. Kind of like carrying you in my pocket. It's going to sound a little weird because I'll be turning the recorder off and on . . .

"Yo, Curious Coop, my man. Where you been, CC? Got your shoes? Listen to this . . ."

Tap, tap, tap, tap . . . tap, tap . . .

"Not bad, Taps. You should have been on Broadway."

"I was on Broadway. Now let's see what you got."

Tap, tap, tap . . . tap, tap, tap, tap . . .

"Whew. You got the juice, CC."

"Who's that?"

"Some girl. Look's like a junkie, wearing shades at night like that."

"She's not a junkie. There's something about her."

"I got bad vibes. Leave her be."

"I'm going to talk to —"

"Too late. She's disappeared into the night."

"I think I've seen her before."

"Forget her . . . By the way, the mayor was asking after you last night. You got her ear. Likes you. I thinks she's gonna take you down."

"That's good news."

(After the tap dance I hear Coop walking for about ten minutes, without a word, as if he's forgotten the tape recorder is in his pocket, then . . .)

"Hi, Meg."

"Evening, Coop."

"You didn't happen to see a girl pass by recently? Street girl — small, wearing shades."

"Didn't see her, but I wasn't looking."

"No big deal. How's Tootsie?"

"See for yourself."

"Has she been eating?"

"Nope. She's not interested. Gettin' old like me I guess."

"Maybe she'll be interested in this. I'll just break off little bits."

"You're a good boy, Coop. Nobody cares about Tootsie and me but you. I found some books in the trash yesterday. Saved them for you."

"You should read them first."

"You know I don't read no more. My eyes."

"How about if I read them out loud to you. I used to read to my brother all the time."

"I ain't no baby that needs story time. Got my own stories runnin' in my head at high speed in high def. Just take the books, you rascal. I gotta be going. It's gonna rain tonight. You gotta place where it's dry?"

"Soon, I might have a place where it never rains . . ."

And that's how it went. Back and forth for several months. I'd send a recording. A few days later Coop would send one back. His were much longer than mine and a lot more interesting until . . .

NOVEMBER IS COLD HERE, PATRICK

but I'm sticking in the city. A lot of people head south for the winter if they can scrape together enough cash. And no, I'm not asking for money. I don't need it. I already have my entrance fee, and it's taken me months to earn it. Keep sending those recordings, and I'll record you back when I can. I have to go now. My guide awaits.

When I first listened to this I didn't think much about it. The only thing that struck me as a little odd was that he called me Patrick. I'm Meatloaf, Lil Bro, Pat, but never Patrick. That would be like me calling him Cooper, which he hated. This all started with my parents, who did not believe in the shortening of given names. My father's name was Bertrand O'Toole, never Bert. My mother's name was Ariel O'Toole, never Ari. To annoy them, Coop took the *er* out of Cooper. And when I was born he took the *rick* out of Patrick.

I replied with another one of my boring recordings.

Then another, and another, and another, then some letters . . .

I've been checking the PO box on the way to school and on the way home.

Empty.

28

No word from Coop.

Here's what Dad said . . .

"So you've been sending recordings back and forth and Cooper is in New York?"

"Yeah. But it's been a month since he sent one back. I think something's happened."

"Maybe he moved on. Maybe his recorder is broken. Maybe he didn't pay the PO box rental fee. Maybe he's just preoccupied . . . you know how he can get."

"Or maybe he's in the hospital."

"A hospital would contact us. He would have to fill out forms. Next of kin, et cetera, someone would call us. He didn't contact you for a year after he left here. What makes you think he wouldn't do that again? And he didn't contact me or your mother at all."

"I think something's happened."

"I think he's fine, but, if you want, I'll file a missing person's report. Now, I need to talk to you about Christmas break."

"What about it?"

"Denise and I are going to Belize to try and find one of the rarest birds in Central America, the keel-billed motmot. I emailed your mom and she said you can spend the holidays in Florida with her."

(Mom and Dad had stopped talking on the phone, because when they did they argued. You can't argue in an email . . . at least not loudly.)

"I don't want —"

"I know, but you can't go with us. We're going to be gone for sixteen days, and you have only two weeks off of school. And we are going to fly. No other way to get to Belize quickly. You can take the train to Florida. I've already bought you a ticket."

"Does Mom really want me in Florida?"

"Absolutely! She misses you, and she wants you to spend some time with your . . . uh . . . potentially anyway . . . step-sisters. If your mom . . . Well, if she marries this guy, those three girls are going to be in your life for the rest of your life."

"You'll check on Coop?"

"First thing tomorrow morning. I'm sure he's fine. Don't worry about him."

BUT I AM WORRIED ABOUT COOP

and the longer it goes without a word from him the more worried I become.

I've lost track of how many recordings I've sent. Two weeks ago I included a self-addressed stamped postcard with a note telling him to send it back to me so I would know if he was okay. All he had to do was drop it in the slot at the post office. It didn't come back. I sent a registered letter he had to sign for. He didn't sign for it. The letter came back. I called the post office in New York and asked a postal worker what they did with regular mail that wasn't picked up. He told me if the letters have return addresses they are sent back to the sender as undeliverable. (All of my unregistered letters and packages had return addresses. None of them have come back.) I asked him if he knew Coop. He said he couldn't tell me, and even if he could, it would be unlikely he would know him anyway. "Kid," he said, "I've been at this post office for over twenty years and I don't even know everyone who works here."

I called the FBI.

I asked for Agent Ryan — the same agent who had showed up at the house when Coop blew up the neighborhood. When she finally got on the phone I was surprised she remembered who I was.

"How's Coop?" she asked. "I haven't heard from him in a long time."

I told her that he was missing and that Dad was going to contact the police in New York.

"Not much else he can do," Agent Ryan said. "Coop's eighteen now. He's probably just out stretching his wings . . . seeing how they work, doing his own thing. Before I joined the FBI I was a New York cop. Finding someone there who doesn't want to be found is nearly impossible."

"I'm worried about him," I said.

"I'll tell you what I'll do," Agent Ryan said. "I'll send a memo to our New York office. Do you have a recent photo?"

"I can email you one taken before he left. I don't know if he looks the same."

"That'll do. I'm sure Coop looks like he's always looked . . . charming. The NYPD has a better chance of running him down than we do, but you never know. One of our people might get lucky and come across him."

"I appreciate it."

"No problem. Like I told you, I like your brother despite his little accident. There's something different about him. You know?"

I knew.

Dad hasn't gotten much further with the cops. He filed a missing person's report, but the detective told him that Coop was a low priority.

"I was on the phone with the detective for over an hour.

And the only reason he spent that much time talking to me was because I dropped the Nobel laureate bomb."

(Dad rarely drops the Nobel laureate bomb. He thinks it's unseemly.)

"He wouldn't tell me how many missing person's reports were filed every day in New York, which led me to believe there were a lot of them. He told me the priorities were children and seniors. I emailed him a couple of photos of Cooper, and he said they would run them against the John Does they have in the morgue. He'll also send Cooper's name to all the hospitals and clinics. That's all he could do. A needle in a haystack was how he put it. He said that most of the time the missing person isn't really missing. They're just hanging out with friends. Or lying low. Or they're out of town. They resurface eventually. If Cooper is in trouble — or if he's injured — there's a chance they'll find him. That's all we can do."

"We could hire a private detective agency."

"I asked him about that too. He told me it was a huge rip-off. Private investigators make a fortune on long shots like this, milking the family for everything they have. I know you're worried about Cooper. He'll show up when he's ready. I'll call that detective when we get back from Belize. Who knows — Cooper might just show up here for Christmas."

"We'll be gone."

"He has a key. Leave him a note. I'm sure he'll stick around until you get back from Florida."

I didn't tell Dad, but . . .

I'M NOT GOING TO FLORIDA

It's Thursday afternoon. December 23.

I'm on a train headed north.

I talked to Mom about Coop.

Her reaction was almost identical to Dad's.

She sounded exhausted and not exactly overjoyed about me coming down for Christmas.

I guess the stay-at-home-mom-with-three-toddlers thing was not nearly as energizing as astrophysics and being an astronaut. She was interviewing for a position at Kennedy Space Center, confident she was going to get it, and said I would be hanging with my three potential half sisters and their full-time nanny during the day.

Right.

It's cold. Frost on the window.

Dad thinks spending two weeks in the rain forest looking for a keel-billed motmot is more important than spending a day in New York City looking for his son. I can't even pretend to know what Mom is thinking. All I know is that neither one of them are thinking about my brother.

Coop is a rare bird too.

I began planning my expedition weeks ago.

Late this morning I wrote an email to Mom from Dad.

Patrick has changed his mind about going to Florida over Christmas. He wants to go to Belize with me. I warned him about the long flight, but he swears it won't be a problem. I hope he's right. Anyway, we'll take him with us. We're heading out in a couple of minutes. Merry Christmas.

After I sent the email I disabled Dad's email account.

I also unplugged the home phone, took the SIM card from his cell, ran hot water over it, then slipped it back into the cell. Oops. No signal.

They dropped me at the train station on their way to the airport.

I exchanged my ticket to Orlando for a ticket to New York City. Got almost two hundred dollars back to add to my stash of cash.

Yesterday I told two friends who can keep their mouths shut what I'm doing just in case something happens and I don't make it back to school on January 3. I gave them Mom's number in Florida, because Dad will still be in Belize, and told them where I'm staying in New York, the Chelsea Star Hotel. It's not far from Coop's post office and it's down the street from Penn Station, which I'll be pulling into in about two hours.

I'll spend the time re-listening to Coop's recordings. Somewhere in them he's told me where he is.

I plug my earphones in.

Ten nights to find him.

TWO

BENEATH

THE POST OFFICE

is crowded. People are standing in line with last-minute packages that will never make it in time for Christmas.

No one pays attention to me as I talk into this recorder. That's because most of them are talking on cell phones or Bluetooths. Some people hanging around the post office talk to themselves without any device. No one pays any attention to them either.

I'll transcribe all this into my journal later. I can see why Coop likes this recorder, but I still prefer writing things down.

PO Box 1611. To me the numbers look like they are on fire, but of course they are just like all the other numbers on the other PO boxes. I just peeked through the keyhole. It looked like there was mail inside.

I walked directly here from Penn Station without checking into the hotel.

I thought: *What if Coop picks up the mail while I'm checking in?*

I realize how stupid this is now. The post office is open 6:00 a.m. to 7:00 p.m. Monday through Friday, and Saturday it will be closed because it's Christmas . . . Coop might have already picked up yesterday's mail, or he could stroll in here at six in the morning, which is more likely . . . creature of the night that he is. That's probably why he didn't sign for the registered letter I sent. There was no one here to give it to him. I can't spend twenty-four hours a day for the next ten days waiting for him to show up.

I have to sleep.

I have to eat.

I have to pee . . .

I'm walking up to one of the homeless people. An old man with a slight limp wearing two coats, a blue neck scarf, and a stocking cap, thumbing through a magazine he just fished out of the trash.

"Hi, do you know where the nearest restroom is?"

"There's one in here, but you can't use it unless you work for the federal friggin' government even though you paid for the toilet with your taxes, but you're too young to pay taxes so you don't know nothin' about that, so your best bet is the sandwich shop half a block down, but they don't like people using the can 'less they buy something . . . cheapest thing there is a hot dog, set you back three bucks, and it's not even a good hot dog, but it will get you into the head. 'Course you're a kid, and dressed okay, so you might be able to waltz right in and use the john without the hot dog."

"Thanks. Say . . . uh . . . I'm here looking for my brother. His name's Coop. A little older than me. Brown curly hair, green eyes, nice smile. Friendly. He has a PO box here. I'm wondering if you know him, or if you've seen him."

"Don't think so. I'm not a regular here. Popped in to get warm and wait for the soup kitchen to open. That old bag standing over in the corner is always hanging around in here. At least, she's been here every time I've loitered in. I think her name is Sadie, or Satan, or something. She's not right in the head, but who is? She might know him. You wouldn't happen to have any cash on you would you? Like enough for a hot dog so I can use the can and get something in my belly before the kitchen opens up. That lousy hot dog is better than the swill they serve at the kitchen."

"Sure." I gave him a five-dollar bill.

"Thanks. Merry friggin' Christmas."

"Sadie?"

"What do you want?"

"Nothing really. I'm just looking for my brother. I hear you know everyone who comes and goes here. His name's Coop. Brown curly hair, green eyes, nice smile."

"I know him. Good kid. Helps people. But he don't ever come in here."

"But he has a post office box here."

"I said he don't ever come in here. I'd know it if he did. Seen him on the street."

"Which street?"

"All over the place. Bump into him every week or two."

"Do you know where he lives?"

"Street kid. Lives where he can, like the rest of us."

"If you see him, can you tell him that his brother, Pat, is looking for him?"

"Who's Pat?"

"Me. I'm his brother."

"I'll tell him if I remember, but there's no guarantee of that. My mind wanders. Can't wrap it around things for long. You got a place to stay?"

"I'm at the Chelsea Star Hotel . . . well, I will be as soon as I check in. He could leave a message for me there."

"So, you got money?"

"A little."

"Well, don't be telling people that. And don't be giving money to people like you just gave that fiver to the scarf man. He's probably an addict. You can tell by the yellow eyes and bones stickin' out all over the place. You give him a fiver, he'll follow you and take the rest of your money after hittin' you in the head, lettin' you freeze to death in the snow. Then your brother will leave you a message that you'll never get. You act like a victim, you'll be a victim. Remember that."

"Coop might come in here late at night. You might have missed him."

"Maybe, but I spend a lot of nights in here and I've never seen him. I'd remember that . . . I think. Looks easy standing here all day, but sometimes I doze off or zone out. He might have slipped in and out in between."

"Well, thanks, Sadie."

"By the way my name ain't Sadie. It's Satin, like the fabric."

I've retaken my position with 1611 in view not sure what to do. Satin seems sharper than she acts. I'm watching her now. Her eyes are darting around, watching everyone and everything. I doubt those eyes miss much. They'd know if Coop came in here.

I still have to pee.

I . . .

Wait . . .

What the . . .

There's a bald man, in his late fifties or early sixties, wearing an expensive-looking overcoat and suit.

He's opening 1611.

He's pulling the mail out.

He has a red day pack slung over his shoulder.

He's stuffing the mail into the pack.

"Excuse me?"

"What?"

"Is 1611 your PO box?"

"What do you think? I have a key. Now go away."

"Do you know Coop O'Toole? I'm his brother, and —"

"I said get outta here. I don't have a handout for you."

"I'm not asking for a handout. Where are you going? Wait. Wait. Wait!"

BUT THE MAN DIDN'T WAIT

He pushed his way through the crowded post office and ran out the door.

I hesitated . . .

That's not accurate.

I froze.

I didn't expect a businessman to open 1611.

I didn't expect him to accuse me of panhandling.

I didn't expect him to run out of the post office in a panic.

Among the letters he stuffed into the red pack, at least one of them was from me. I recognized the purple envelope.

By the time I grabbed my backpack and got outside, the man was half a block away. Hurrying. I saw the top of his bald head disappear down the steps to the subway. I ran after him. At the bottom of the steps I had another delay at a vending machine to buy a MetroCard so I could get through the turnstile.

People were piling into a train as I reached the platform. I didn't see the man. I had no idea if he had gotten on this train or managed to catch the one before it.

I squeezed on just before the doors slid closed.

It was so crowded I wouldn't have been able to see the man if he was standing five feet away.

I still had to pee.

But I had a worse problem.

Claustrophobia.

I had trotted down the stairs and jumped on the car without even thinking about it.

My chest tightened. I broke into a cold sweat. I closed my eyes. I tried to breathe.

Claustrophobia. Fear of enclosed spaces, fear of restriction, fear of suffocation, leading to panic attacks.

This is the only scar I have from the tunnel collapse. I always sleep with a window open no matter how cold it is outside. I avoid crowded, confined spaces, like airplanes, which is why I couldn't fly to Belize with Dad and Denise.

Trains are fine because I can get up and move around.

I guess crowded subway cars aren't the same as trains.

You learn something new every day.

I was having a panic attack.

I didn't care about Coop or the man. All I cared about was getting off that car.

It didn't help that I was facing five panels that read:

EVACUATION INSTRUCTIONS

LISTEN FOR DIRECTIONS FROM
AUTHORIZED PERSONNEL.

REMAIN INSIDE TRAIN IF POSSIBLE.
IF NOT . . .

GO TO NEXT CAR THROUGH END DOORS.

IF UNABLE . . .

OPEN SIDE DOOR AND GO OUT.

IF UNABLE . . .

GO OUT EMERGENCY WINDOWS.

Next to the evacuation instructions was another sign:

EMERGENCY EXIT

1. PULL HANDLE. 2. REMOVE RUBBER. 3. REMOVE WINDOW.

I was about to skip all three steps and kick the window out, but the car slowed and stopped at the next station.

I stumbled onto the platform gasping for breath.

I puked.

When I looked up I saw the businessman again.

He was turning a corner, heading back up to the street.

I wiped my mouth.

I wasn't going to lose him again.

Unless he got on another subway car.

THE DAY PACK

was like a red beacon.

It led me uptown to the New York Public Library.

The man went inside but was there for only ten minutes before he came back out.

I followed him two more blocks.

He disappeared into a fitness club.

There was a restaurant across the street and that meant a restroom. I hurried over to it, asked for a window table, hit the urinal, washed my hands and face, then brushed my teeth to get the sour taste out of my mouth.

I ordered a personal flatbread cheese-and-mushroom pizza and a Coke. Sixteen bucks. A skinny waiter brought me my six-fifty-a-slice pizza and three-dollar Coke. Overall, my first few hours in the city could not have gone better, discounting the panic attack and puking, but even that worked out. If I'd gone to the hotel to check in, I probably would have missed the suit with the key. If I hadn't had the panic attack, I probably would have stayed on the subway through a couple more stops and would have missed him completely.

While I ate, I watched the entrance of the fitness club and glanced at my NYC map, which I had almost memorized. I was happy to see that I knew exactly where I was in relationship to Penn Station and the hotel, because I was going to have to follow the guy. He had the key to the PO box, and the box was the only direct link I had to Coop.

I dug another coat out of my pack and switched it with the one I'd been wearing to throw him off in case he was watching for me.

The waiter cleared my plate and glass, and I walked out into the cold and waited in an alley to keep out of the wind. I had to move from my shelter twice to make room for delivery trucks — Mack's Meats, and about twenty minutes later, a second truck, Cloud's Mushrooms.

The man had been in the club for over an hour.

It was dark out now. Not many people on the street. Maybe I missed him leaving. Maybe he knew I was following him and slipped out a different door. Maybe he worked at the club and wasn't going anywhere. Maybe . . .

An old man came out of the club with a red day pack over his shoulder, but he wasn't dressed anything like the old man who walked into the club. He was wearing baggy jeans and a black hooded sweatshirt that had seen better days. The hood was pulled over his bald head, but he was the right height, he moved like the old guy I was following, and there was a red day pack slung over his shoulder.

"Decide," I told myself.

I FOLLOWED HIM

But with every step he took I thought I had made a mistake.

It couldn't possibly be the same man.

He stopped half a block down and rummaged through a garbage can, shook out a plastic grocery bag, and dropped in what looked like a half-eaten sandwich.

A block later he ducked into an alley. I didn't follow him because he'd see me, but I heard him rummaging again. A few minutes later he emerged with more stuff in the plastic bag.

And this is how it went, block after block.

His garbage-picking was not random.

He was following a definite route.

He'd done this countless times before.

After two hours he was holding two stuffed bags in each hand and a third tied to the red pack slung over his shoulder. He had enough food to feed himself for a week.

But why?

I wanted to confront him again and ask him about Coop and the PO box, and to make sure it was the same guy, but I was afraid he might run off again. So I just followed him zigzagging through the cold city from garbage can to garbage can, Dumpster to Dumpster. He would have to stop foraging eventually. And he did . . .

At about ten o'clock he went down yet another alley.

I waited across the street, hands in my pockets, jumping up and down, trying to keep warm, waiting for him to come back out.

He didn't.

Maybe he went out the other side . . . although he hadn't when he'd gone into any of the other alleys. Maybe he lived in the alley and was stuffing his face before he went to sleep.

Maybe I was afraid to walk into the dark alley and check.

This was more like it.

And it had nothing to do with claustrophobia. Dark alleys are not on my claustrophobic list. But they are on my chicken list. Especially when there's a garbage picker lurking in the shadows. I tried to convince myself that the man was more afraid of me than I was of him. When he was in his suit he had run away from me. But now he wasn't in a suit.

What would Coop do?

That made me laugh.

Coop would stroll into that alley like it was his own bedroom, with that idiotic grin on his face ready for anything that waited for him in the dark.

I wasn't Coop, and I sure wasn't grinning, but I walked into that dark alley.

RATS

I couldn't see them, but I could hear them squeaking and skittering as I called out ridiculously . . .

"Hello? Hello? It's Coop's brother, Pat. I'm not here to cause a problem. I just want to talk."

The alley was about a hundred feet long and ended in a solid brick wall. There was only one door. It had bars over it and was locked from the outside with a bulletproof padlock. The closest windows were twenty feet up.

No fire escape.

No Dumpster.

No guy.

Poof!

He had vanished.

UP EARLY

and out on the street after the late night transcribing the recordings into my journal.

First stop: the alley.

If this is where he vanished, this is where he would have to reappear.

Right?

Wrong.

The big padlock on the barred door was rusty and hadn't been opened in years. I couldn't even tell how the rats got out of the alley — I didn't see a big enough chink in the bricks for them to squeeze through.

He may have vanished into thin air, but I doubted he was going to suddenly materialize out of thin air. And I didn't think he was going to show up at the post office after what had happened there yesterday.

That left me with the fitness club and the restaurant across the street.

THE SAME SKINNY WAITER

brought me my breakfast.

A cheese-and-mushroom omelet, three sausage links, toast, orange juice (from concentrate). Twenty-two dollars and fifty-three cents without the tip. If I sat there through dinner waiting for the guy to show up at the club, a third of my cash would be gone. Maybe this explained why the guy was Dumpster diving the night before. You need a lot of money to survive in New York City.

I rehearsed my next move as I ate. It was a big fitness club, but they had to know this guy well. How many people come into the club in a suit, work out, then leave as a homeless person?

Being young has some advantages.

And the time of year wouldn't hurt either.

As soon as I finished my last three-dollar sausage link (burnt) I was going to walk over to the club and tell them the mystery man was my long-lost father and that my mother and I wanted him home for Christmas.

I didn't think they'd give me his address or phone number. But I was hoping they'd at least tell me how often he came to the club and at what time. They might even give me his name. After all, it was almost Christmas.

*　　*　　*

I dropped twenty-five dollars on the table and was about to leave the restaurant when I saw the man with the red day pack cross the street and walk into the club.

I sat down, ordered another four-dollar OJ, and waited.

He was back out within a half hour dressed just like he was at the post office the day before — except he was wearing a red tie instead of a blue tie.

Two blocks later he walked into a bank.

I tried to follow him in, but I was stopped by a security guard.

"Bank's not open yet."

"Oh . . . uh . . . I saw Mr. uh . . ."

"Mr. Trueman?"

"Right. I saw Mr. Trueman walk in and thought . . ."

"Come back when the bank opens."

"Great. I'll come back then."

I crossed the street and went into a Walgreens and came out with a disposable cell phone. I should have bought one the night before. Now at least I could call 911 if I needed to, but more important, I could call the bank. I called information and dialed the number.

"May I speak to Mr. Trueman?"

"I'm afraid new accounts isn't open yet. You'll have to call back at nine."

I DID NOT CALL BACK

I walked into the bank at nine with my recorder on.

"Hi, I need to open a new account. I'm supposed to talk to a Mr. Trueman."

"Terry's right over there at his desk."

"Thanks . . . Hi, Terry."

"What are you doing here?"

"Like I told you yesterday at the post office, I'm looking for my brother, Coop."

"And like I told you, I don't know your brother. I'm going to call security."

"Do that. And I'll tell everyone here about your other life."

"I don't know what you're talking about."

"The fitness club, the old clothes, Dumpster diving, the alley."

"You followed me to the alley last night?"

"Yeah."

"Sit down. Act like you're filling out this form . . . I don't know what your game is, but we can't talk here . . . There's a coffee shop on the corner. I'll meet you there in twenty minutes."

I waited outside the bank where Terry couldn't see me and watched the entrance.

I didn't trust him.

When I'd said hi he'd nearly come out of his suit.

I was sure there was a back door to the bank, but I couldn't be in two places at once.

But he walked out the front door, obviously nervous, and hurried down the street to the coffee shop. I followed him inside and switched the recorder on as I sat down across from him . . .

"What's it going to take?"

"What do you mean?"

"How much to keep your mouth shut?"

"I don't want any money. I'm just looking for my brother."

"So you weren't going to blow the whistle on me back at the bank?"

"No. I just said that so you'd talk to me."

"You're saying I can end this conversation right now, go back to the bank, and you won't come in and tell everyone about . . . What did you call it? My other life . . ."

"What would be the point?"

"So this is legit. You're not shaking me down. Coop's really your brother."

"Yeah. Have you seen him? Do you know where he is?"

"He never said he had a brother."

"He never says much of anything about himself."

"Let's see some ID."

"See? Same last name."

"Tell me what he looks like. Describe him."

"I haven't seen him in a year, but he's a little under six

feet, brown curly hair, green eyes, always smiling. He looks a little like me, but I'm shorter, and my hair's black. My eyes are blue."

"I see the family resemblance."

"Where is Coop?"

"Let's talk about the alley first."

"What about it? Which alley?"

"The last one. The one you didn't come out of. I went back there this morning. You didn't use the entrance?"

"No, I —"

"Thank God! We're not supposed to use the same entrance twice in a row. There are rules. You're lucky you didn't go down."

"What rules? Down where?"

"You don't know anything, do you?"

"I guess not. Tell me about Coop."

"You're not from here. Did you run away?"

"Not exactly. I mean . . . uh . . . my parents are gone for the holiday. They don't know I'm here. I came to New York to see if I could find Coop. We haven't heard from him in a while. You picked up a couple of my letters to him yesterday."

"I'm the postman. I just drop off the letters and packages and pick up the mail. I can't tell you if Coop got them or not. It would be best if you went back home. This isn't any place for a kid like you."

"I'm not going back until I find Coop."

"You'll have to talk to May."

"Who's May?"

"Do you have a sleeping bag?"

"No, I'm staying in a hotel."

"Get one, get a sleeping bag. I'll meet you outside the fitness club at six. Don't be late. We have a lot to do. If you're not there, I'm gone."

THE NIGHT BEFORE CHRISTMAS

and I'm back at the restaurant waiting for a banker to trot up the stairs to the fitness center and morph into a homeless person.

Mr. Terry Trueman.

Homeless for the holidays.

This might be the strangest Christmas Eve I've ever spent, and that's saying something, because all my Christmas Eves and Christmas Days have been a little odd.

Coop started the tradition.

Even when he was a little kid he didn't want things. Mom said that we still had wrapped Christmas/birthday presents (they celebrated his birthday and Christmas on the same day) up in the attic from when Coop was two years old. He refused to open them, which kind of ruined the gift-exchange thing. The only exception was the tap shoes I'd given him.

Mom and Dad, being scientists, were happy to buy into the let's-not-make-a-big-deal-out-of-Christmas thing. They weren't complete grinches, but they didn't do the decorated tree, stockings over the fireplace, Christmas lights, or any of the other trappings. Most years we'd leave town and stay in a nice hotel somewhere. New York twice. Or we'd go to someplace warm. I should say that we *cruised* to someplace warm. (After I was nine there were no more airplanes for me.)

Even though Coop didn't come right out and say it on the recordings, I knew he was flirting with the underground again, which has me a little worried as I sit here writing in this journal.

Or maybe it wasn't *again*.

Maybe he had never stopped.

Maybe all those nights he left our house with his shoes hanging around his neck he wasn't tapping.

I put the earphones in and fast-forwarded to Coop's references to what lies below:

There are over 700 miles of subway tunnels beneath New York. In 1912 the workers digging the Brooklyn-Manhattan Transit subway accidentally rediscovered the city's very first subway line, forty-two years after it closed . . .

Buried under Front Street is an 18th-century merchant ship, 25 feet wide and 92 feet long. The bow of the ship was cut off and is now on display in Newport News, Virginia. The stern is still under the street . . .

Beneath Chrystie Street is a six-lane highway built in the late 1960s, then sealed and forgotten . . . .

Below the theater district are dozens of public toilets that haven't been tinkled in for years . . .

Several stories under the Waldorf Astoria hotel is a private entrance that allowed President Franklin D. Roosevelt secret passage to the private train carrying him to and from his home in Hyde Park . . .

The people who live beneath the streets are called Mole

People, but they don't like that name. Some say there are over two thousand of them . . .

The rats under the city are called track rabbits, because they are sometimes eaten during lean times . . .

A place where it never rains . . .

And no, I'm not asking for money. I don't need it. I already have my entrance fee, and it's taken me months to earn it. Keep sending those recordings, and I'll record you back when I can. I have to go now. My guide awaits.

MY GUIDE AWAITS TOO

He's walking into the fitness club.

This is insane.

I don't even know this guy.

But Coop must have trusted him.

I bought a sleeping bag and some other stuff at an outdoor store.

When this guy comes out he's taking me beneath.

Just twenty-four hours ago I had a panic attack on a subway.

How am I going to react now?

If there was an entrance in that alley I sure didn't see it.

Mr. Trueman's coming back out of the club wearing his black hooded sweatshirt, tattered overcoat, jeans, boots, and gloves.

I'm closing my journal.

Time to go.

I HAD TO JOG

to catch up with him.

"I didn't think you'd show," he said, walking down the street in the opposite direction he had gone the night before. "I wish you hadn't. Did you get a sleeping bag?"

I could see his breath in the cold.

"Yeah."

We walked for three blocks, then turned down an alley.

"Good pickings here. Even better on Christmas Eve. The restaurant isn't open tonight, and it'll be closed all weekend. They toss the good stuff."

He flipped open the lid to a metal Dumpster with a bang. Four rats scurried out from under the Dumpster.

"Track rabbits," I said.

"You mean rats," Mr. Trueman said.

"Coop called them track rabbits."

"Are you nuts? We don't eat rats. And you better stay clear of them. Guy I knew got swarmed a few years ago. Not much left when the meal was over, and the guy wasn't the one doing the eating." He pulled a handful of plastic grocery bags out of his pack and handed half of them to me. "Here are the rules. Only take things that haven't been gnawed on by humans or rats. Give it the sniff test. If it smells funky, don't put it in your bag."

"Funky?"

"That's right. Tainted. Rotten. Odd. Foul. Corrupt. Diseased. Spoiled. If it's not something you'd eat raw if you didn't have a fire to cook it, throw it away."

He climbed into the Dumpster.

I stood where I was.

"What are you waiting for? You can't pick unless you're in the pile. And don't think Coop didn't pick. He showed me this Dumpster. In fact, I'm takin' you on his route. He had a knack. You can't believe some of the things he found."

I climbed in.

"This is the most wasteful city on earth. The food thrown away here every day is enough to feed entire countries for a month. But you gotta know where to look. That restaurant you came out of across from the club is not one of the places to look. You paid for food that I wouldn't take for free."

I touched something deep in the pile.

It was cold and soft.

Something dead.

I closed my eyes as I pulled it out.

"Beautiful!" Mr. Trueman took it from me. "Eighteen pounds give or take." He sniffed it. "Fresh. You know how many families right here in the city can't afford a turkey dinner for Christmas? Tens of thousands that's how many. And you just plucked one for absolutely nothing from one of the best restaurants in the city."

"I don't get it."

"Me either, but that's just the way it is."

"I'm not talking about the turkey, Mr. Trueman."

"Drop the Mr. Trueman. That's not my real name anyway. You can call me Terry or Posty. Those aren't my real names either. Now what don't you get?"

"Why are you doing this? You have a job. You make money."

Posty picked through more trash, finding a bag filled with croutons. "Stuffing. You mean Dumpster diving?"

"Right. Why are you doing this if you have a job?"

"It started with a two-thousand-dollar suit."

"What?"

"I'm not kidding. We find all sorts of things going through the trash. We eat the food, but if we find something like a two-thousand-dollar suit we take it to a secondhand store, or we try to sell it on the street. Anyway, almost twenty years ago now I found a beautiful suit zipped up in a suit bag in a Dumpster. The tailor's name was right on the bag, so I thought I might get the best price by taking it back to him. I'm walking down the street with the bag slung over my shoulder and I start thinking about what I'm carrying. I go into a public restroom and try it on. It was a perfect fit. And I mean perfect. I looked like a millionaire except for my shirt and shoes. So instead of taking it back to the tailor I go to a secondhand shop and buy a pair of shoes, a white shirt, and a red power tie. I think that suit made me go temporarily insane, because I walked into a stylist shop for a haircut, shave, and manicure that cost me more money than I'd usually spent in a year back then.

"When I come out I *buy* a *New York Post* with the last of my change. I read the newspaper most days, but I had never in my life *bought* one. So now I'm completely broke, but I look like I own the city. I go through the employment listings and see they're looking for a bank trainee. I know the bank. It's right next door to a restaurant with a great Dumpster in back.

"I walk into the bank, and everyone there is fawning all over me. I mean they thought I owned the bank. I tell them that I'm interested in the trainee job. I fill out an application with absolute lies. The bank president interviews me and hires me on the spot. I didn't think I'd show up for the job . . . It was just one of those I-wanted-to-see-if-I-could-do-it things. But I walk in on Monday in my suit, and twenty years later I'm still there."

"So you have an apartment. You don't live . . . uh . . . beneath."

Posty looked at me a second. "I don't have an apartment. Why would I want an apartment where I would have to pay rent, utility bills, phone bills, and have neighbors I don't even know?"

"What do you do with the money you make at the bank?"

"Not much. Fitness club dues. I buy a suit once in a while, shirts, socks, shoes . . . all used. Most months I make enough money from the stuff I find on the street for everything I need. I put the money I make from the bank in the bank. Not the bank I'm working at — I don't want them to know how much I have. I don't need the job or the money. I work at the bank because I like the people there and I'm good at what I do. Mr. Trueman has made some very sound investments, and someday he's going to use his money to help people out. He just hasn't decided exactly how to do this yet."

We climbed out of the Dumpster.

"So you're a homeless banker."

"I'm a banker, but I'm not homeless. I'm *houseless*, and there's a difference between the two. There was a time when I was homeless, but that was years ago."

HE HANDED ME THE EIGHTEEN-POUND TURKEY

to carry as we walked down the frosty street.

"Christmas Eve. We'll be hauling a lot of stuff tonight — last chance for a couple of days. Everything will be closed down tomorrow. But next week things will really pick up. You wouldn't believe what the department stores throw away after Christmas. Then there's the New Year. Everyone dumps the junk they got in the previous year to make room for the junk they're going to get in the New Year. I've actually picked things out of Dumpsters and sold them to the same people who dumped them the day before. And they say people like me are crazy."

We got to an alley near an Italian restaurant. I started to turn down it.

"Not that one," Posty said.

"There's a Dumpster," I said.

"A bad-luck Dumpster. Keep walking. I found something horrible in that Dumpster one night. In fact, it was Christmas Eve almost twenty years ago. I haven't been down that alley since."

"What was it?"

"I'm not telling you. It's bad enough that I have it seared

in my mind. I don't even like walking by this alley. A day doesn't go by that I don't think about it. Let's go."

We arrived at the next Dumpster and climbed inside.

"So Coop did this with you?"

"Sometimes. But mostly he worked on his own. Night owl. Stayed out on the streets long after I was in bed. He was a natural scrounger. The kid could find anything. That's how he got his ticket beneath. That and the fact that he was likable and wasn't an addict or a thief. He was pretty quiet. Didn't say much. Just sat back and took everything in. May liked him right away."

That was Coop, but I didn't like the fact that he was talking about Coop in the past tense.

"Who's May?"

"I guess I better explain the names. May's in charge of the Community. She's our mayor."

"And you're Posty because you pick up the mail?"

"Right. Sparks is our electrician. TV is our cable and TV guy. Plum is our plumber. Chef is our cook. Handy is our builder. IT is our computer guy. Vet is our doctor."

"He's a veteran?"

"No. He used to be a veterinarian, but he's also a pretty good human doc. The point is most of us have nicknames related to our jobs."

"So you have to have a skill to be in the Community."

"Not necessarily, but you have to bring something to the plate. In addition to delivering and picking up the mail, which is only a part-time job, I'm also a scrounger, with food as a specialty. Coop was on his way to becoming a scrounger too."

"What do you mean 'was'?"

"This Dumpster's a bust. Let's go to the next one."

WE WENT TO TWO MORE DUMPSTERS

before he told me what he meant by "was."

Sort of.

"Right now there are twenty-three permanent members of the Community and a handful of what we call visitors. Coop was a visitor, which isn't what it sounds like. To become a visitor you have to be invited to the Community by one of the permanent members, and we can only invite one visitor a year. And most of us don't invite any visitors at all because there's a risk involved."

"What's that?"

"Banishment. If we bring someone below who disrupts the Community, we might get voted out of the Community. It's happened before. So we're careful about who we invite."

"So someone can't just drop in?"

Posty laughed. "Impossible. No one can find us."

"What about the visitors?"

"Blindfolded in and out every day, every night, every time. They are met above and escorted beneath."

"I'm going to be blindfolded?"

"If you want to go beneath, absolutely."

My chest started to tighten just at the thought of being blindfolded and escorted beneath.

"You okay?"

I took a deep breath.

"I'm fine."

But I wasn't.

I was scared.

"You said that Coop was on his way to becoming a scrounger. What happened?"

"Here's how it works. After a month the permanent members of the Community vote on whether the visitor can join the Community. It has to be unanimous. We don't discuss the pros and cons. We don't try to persuade or influence each other. It's a simple yes or no written on a scrap of paper tossed into a bucket. One no and the visitor is escorted above and is never allowed to visit the Community again."

"So Coop got a no."

"Nope. He got twenty-two yeses. In fact, another guy and I were going to put him up for membership, but May beat us to it. I liked him too. Coop's a permanent member of the Community. Number twenty-three. But after he was accepted, he had a little different path in mind, which I can't tell you about because I wasn't his sponsor."

"What do you mean?"

"May invited him down. She's the one you need to talk to."

"All I want to know is if Coop is okay."

"You'll have to talk to May."

This was not the answer I wanted, but it was clear that this was the only answer Posty was going to give.

THE LAST DUMPSTER

was a bonanza.

It was like someone had gotten everything ready for the holidays, then at the very last minute, decided to throw Christmas away. Even if Posty had more to tell me about Coop he wouldn't have been able to. He was too excited about the unopened boxes of Christmas lights, candy, ornaments, tinsel, fruitcake, and . . .

"Look at this! It's a complete Santa suit with black boots, belt, hat . . . everything!"

"How are we going to haul all of this stuff?"

We already had more than we could carry.

"Three blocks down is a Thai restaurant. In back of it is an apartment building." He fished a key ring with two keys out of his pocket. "The brass key opens the basement door. The silver key opens a storage locker. Number eight. Right inside the locker door are two grocery carts."

The storage locker was filled with boxes and shelves of junk. I wheeled the carts out of the basement and jogged back to the Dumpster. Posty had everything pulled out and stacked in piles. We filled the carts and wheeled them back to the locker.

"We'll take what we need and leave the rest here. This is just one of our storage areas. If we don't have time to sell what we find, or we can't get the right price, we stash it here or in other lockers we have around the city." He paused and stared at the boxes for a moment, then shook his head. "IT is setting up a system to sell the stuff on eBay." He frowned. "My banking days are numbered. I'll have to become a full-time postman."

"Do you want to?"

"Not really."

"Then why don't you just move above? Lead a regular life."

"And leave the Community? I'd never do that."

"How long have you lived beneath?"

"Twenty-five years, give or take a few months. What are you staring at? There are people who have lived beneath forty years. There are people who have never been on top."

"They had to be born on top."

"What makes you think that?"

IT STARTED TO SNOW

Hard.

We trudged down the street like two houseless Santas with huge black garbage bags slung over our shoulders.

Posty told me how the Community was formed.

"May, Taps, Sparks, and a couple of us had been talking about getting organized for years. But you know how it goes . . . it was just talk. We didn't do anything about it. Our houses were flimsy but livable — nailed together with whatever we could find. There were the druggies and alcoholics and thieves and hooligans coming and going, getting out of the cold or hiding from the cops. It got a little rough sometimes, but we managed. Then 9/11 happened. That changed everything. The transit authority, city cops, and the feds came down and booted us out."

"Why?"

"Because most of the infrastructure of New York City lies underground. If some wacko terrorist planted a couple of bombs beneath, it could kill thousands of people.

"They offered us free apartments and job-training programs, but some of us didn't want to go. May argued that we knew the underground better than the authorities could ever know it. If they left us in place, we would be able to tell them if something was going on. *Homeless* Security, she called it. *Homeland* Security didn't get the joke. They sealed the entries and put up security cameras to make sure they weren't reopened.

"Of course they had no idea where all the entries were, and none of us volunteered the information. We tore our houses down, moved into apartments miles from each other, and fourteen of us were back under the streets within a week. We went deeper. We found a place to rebuild that no one could find. We set up some ground rules . . . or I should say underground rules. We finally got organized."

Posty stopped and started looking through his little red day pack.

"Let me tell you the difference between a house and a home. A house, or a condo, or an apartment are structures. A home is family and has absolutely nothing to do with what it's made of or where it is. Which do you want? The hood or the blindfold?"

"What?"

He held up a black hood in one hand and a black bandanna in the other.

I CHOSE THE BLINDFOLD

but I didn't want either.

"Sorry to make you nervous, but we have rules. We wouldn't last a week if we took visitors down without the blindfold. Someone would tell someone and they would tell someone else and pretty soon a SWAT team would be knocking on our door with sledgehammers."

"I understand," I said.

But what Posty didn't understand was that I wasn't nervous about the blindfold he had just tied around my head. I was nervous about going beneath.

"It's a lot warmer below."

He said this because my knees were shaking.

My knees weren't shaking because it was cold.

"Just put your left hand on my shoulder, and I'll lead you to the entrance."

We walked for a long time with our plastic Christmas bags bumping against our backs. I didn't know if we were walking down different streets or around the same block over and over again.

I didn't care.

The walk gave me a chance to prepare myself. If I had a panic attack, Posty would disappear down the hole like a rabbit, alone, and not pop back up until after New Year's.

"Okay," he said. "We're here. Take your backpack off. I'll follow you down with the bags. Careful. It's a tight squeeze."

Down.

Tight.

Squeeze.

These are not the words a claustrophobic wants to hear.

"You sure you're all right?"

"I'm fine. Just a little cold."

I was sweating in the snow.

"Best to go down headfirst. I'll crawl in behind you."

Crawl.

"No cheating. Keep the blindfold on."

He pushed down on my shoulders.

I got on my knees.

He placed my hands on the edge of the entrance.

"Feel it?"

"Yeah."

"Just stick your head inside and wiggle through."

Inside.

Wiggle.

"It slopes downward. Go slow. When you feel an edge in front of you, stop. There's about a three-foot drop. You'll have to ease yourself to the bottom by bracing yourself on the wall opposite the hole."

I could barely hear him above the sound of my jackhammering heart.

I stuck my head inside and gagged.

"It's not a sewer. Stagnant water. You'll get used to it. It's only a short . . ."

I didn't hear the rest.

Coop hung on to me with blistered hands.

He didn't let go.

He blew his breath into my lungs.

Coop saved my life.

I slithered into the hole like an earthworm being stalked by a robin.

I moved so quickly I missed the edge.

And fell.

Landed on my back in icy water.

Gasping.

Sucking in corrupted air.

SOMETHING HEAVY

landed on my chest.

A giant rat?

A bat?

A second monster landed on top of me.

I fought them off.

I heard a splash.

"You're wrecking our stuff!" Posty grabbed my coat and pulled me to my feet. "What's the matter with you? You're all wet. Do you want to get hypothermia and die?"

"I slipped."

"Be more careful. It's dangerous down here."

He helped me into my backpack.

He handed me one of the plastic bags I had mistaken for a nightmare.

I hoped it was dark and he couldn't see how embarrassed I was. Not that I could see anything myself.

"There isn't enough room here for us to walk side by side. You'll have to hold on to my bag and follow. And watch your footing. We'll take it slow. It's slippery through here, and there are a lot of things to trip over."

The blindfold actually helped.

Not being able to see allowed me to imagine that I was in an open area much bigger than it probably was. Except for my initial panic and my fistfight with the bags, it was going better than I'd expected. I can't say I was relaxed, but I wasn't hyperventilating. And Posty was right about the smell: The worst of it was quickly behind us.

I'm not sure how far or how long we walked, but it seemed like hours. The straps on my pack dug into my shoulders. Every few steps I had to switch the bag to my other hand.

There were a lot of right and left turns.

Posty must have had a flashlight or headlamp, but I could not see the beam.

Subway trains roared past — sometimes close, sometimes far away.

Cars passed overhead.

Water dripped.

Steam hissed.

Every once in a while Posty stopped and took things out of my bag or his and put them into what sounded like trash cans.

"What are you doing?"

"Making deposits. We'll be there in about twenty minutes. You're lucky. That was one of the closer entrances. Some of the outlying entrances can add an hour or more to the trip."

"Do other people in the Community have jobs on the outside like you?"

"A few of them. I'm really going to miss the bank when IT gets that eBay thing going."

"Maybe you can trade your postal job with one of the other members."

"Maybe."

Or maybe you could move up top, I thought, *and lead a normal life.* "Has anyone ever left the Community?"

"Sure. It's not a prison. Half our people are away for the holidays right now. They'll be back after New Year's."

"Where do they go?"

"Visit relatives, kids, parents. Where else would you go for the holidays?"

"Skiing, Disneyland, cruise to someplace warm . . ."

"None of that stuff. They leave to check on the people they know up top. We have a Community kitty that everyone contributes to. If someone has to travel, they can take what they need to get there, but most of us stick around."

"That sounds a lot like rent," I said.

"Well it's not. Up top, rent is mandatory. Beneath, the kitty is voluntary. No one keeps track of who puts money in or how much they put in."

We walked for a while longer, then Posty came to a stop.

"That's interesting."

"What?"

"There's a dog tied up outside the compound. No one in the Community has a dog."

A door opened and we walked through.

It was warmer inside.

The door closed.

He took off my blindfold.

"We're here."

HERE

was a small square room, like a mudroom. Coats and hats hung on the wall. Old shoes and boots were lined up in a neat row on the floor beneath them.

A single bulb dangled from the ceiling. It wasn't bright, but I still had to blink several times to adjust to the light after the blindfold.

Water dripped from some of the coats.

Some of the shoes were wet.

"We don't allow shoes or coats inside because they track in dirt and germs."

Posty opened a second door.

"Come on in and meet the gang."

The room was huge and circular, covered with mismatched carpet, sofas, chairs, and two long dining tables side by side with place settings, including cloth napkins.

There were more than a dozen doors — different sizes, different types, cut into the walls.

Along one curve was a kitchen. Double oven, commercial grill, stainless-steel sink, refrigerator, prep table, and a man dicing onions without looking down at his blurring blade.

Chef?

Twelve sets of eyes stared at me.

One set wore big sunglasses.

A girl.

Short black hair.

Pale skin.

Small.

Older than me, but far younger than the other eleven.

The room was lit but too dim for sunglasses.

No one spoke.

They took me in.

I took in the rest of the circle.

Hundreds of books, magazines, and newspapers piled haphazardly on shelves and tables.

A television mounted to the ceiling was on. The volume muted.

A man sat at a table with three computers.

IT?

Sitting next to the pale girl with the sunglasses was a woman with gray hair.

She spoke first.

May?

I turned on the recorder in my pocket . . .

"Your first visitor, Posty."

"This is Pat O'Toole."

"Coop's little brother?"

"I didn't know Coop had a brother."

"Well he does. And he's here. I checked his ID, and you can see the family resemblance."

"How'd he find you?"

"Are you sure it's his brother?"

"I'm sure. He staked out the post office box."

"Smart, just like Coop."

"Where is Coop?"

"Didn't you tell him?"

"I told him he wasn't here. He wanted more information. Who's the girl?"

"May's keeping it a secret until we are all here. Very mysterious. Her dog is tied up outside."

"I saw it."

"I'll tell all of you who she is, or who I think she is, after dinner."

I WASN'T HUNGRY

but everyone else was.

And talkative.

Except for the girl with sunglasses.

She sat at May's side and said nothing.

She didn't touch the food.

No one talked to me.

I imagined Coop sitting there for the first time.

I bet everyone talked to him.

And by the time the meal was over he knew all their life stories.

But they knew virtually nothing about him.

They liked him just because he was sitting there.

He should have been a cop.

Or a Catholic priest. Lucifer would have spilled his guts to Coop.

"We'll put those Christmas lights up after dinner," Sparks said. "Make it festive for tomorrow."

"I'll start that turkey first thing in the morning," Chef said. "Beautiful bird. Kosher. Not frozen. Clean. Nice find, Posty."

"Pat found it."

"Nice going, kid."

"Did you get an inventory of our stash, Posty? I got the eBay account all set up. We'll be able to get some of the things we need for here off eBay, but we need to build up the balance in our PayPal account before we can bid. We'll need photos of everything for the auctions. Have you started on that?"

"I'll try next week, but it'll be hard, because the pickings are going to be good, like they are after every Christmas . . ."

And this is how the conversation went.

Catching up, mild ribbing, but Community business was always at the center.

The dinner seemed to go on forever.

All I wanted was to find out about Coop.

His name did not come up.

The subject was carefully avoided.

So was the mystery girl with the sunglasses.

Chef brought over a cake and sliced it into thirteen even pieces.

Coffee, tea, milk, and bottled water were poured.

The girl ate her cake.

I was close to completely losing it.

"Let's start with the girl," May said. "I found her outside our door this afternoon. She hasn't spoken. In fact, I don't know if she can speak. I believe she's from the Deep."

Every fork stopped.

They stared at the girl as if she were from another planet.

For nearly a minute there was total silence.

Then everyone started talking at once.

"They'll come looking for her."

"If she hasn't spoken, how do you know she's from the Deep?"

"She can't stay here."

"We'll have to send her back."

"How'd she find us?"

"There will be retributions."

"They'll come tomorrow."

"They might come tonight. Depends on how long she's been gone."

"They can see in the dark."

"They have vicious tracking dogs."

The girl continued eating her cake, seemingly unaware that everyone was talking about her.

"Who are *they*?" I asked.

ALL EYES

shifted to me.

Except for the girl's. She was trying to spear the last cake crumb off her plate.

I pushed my untouched cake over to her.

"Those who have never been above," May answered.

The girl started eating my cake.

"What do you mean?"

"I mean they have always been below. Bred and born in the Deep. Most of them have never seen the sun or the moon or the sky."

"That can't be true."

"It's true. And Posty could not have chosen a worse time to bring you beneath, but of course he didn't know about the girl."

"I'll lead him back up first thing tomorrow morning. No. I better take him up tonight. Tomorrow might be too late."

"I'm not going anywhere. I came down here to find Coop."

"He's not here."

"I figured that. Posty told me I had to talk to you to find out where he is."

"I know where he went, but I don't know where he is."

"I'm sick of these riddles. Where is my brother?"

COOP IS IN THE DEEP

according to May.

Maybe.

I talked her into letting me stay, at least for the night. Early tomorrow morning Posty is taking me back up top.

Maybe.

I'm transcribing the recordings into my journal right now.

The room I'm in is ten by twelve feet.

I'm sitting on Coop's surplus army cot.

There's no bedding. I guess that's why Posty had me get a sleeping bag.

There are wooden crates stacked up along one wall with a few of his favorite flashlights and headlamps, cans of tuna, unopened letters . . . all of them from me.

Things he's gathered from up top.

Dozens of books, including *Dracula* and *A Journey to the Center of the Earth*.

His tap shoes are nowhere to be seen.

He wouldn't have taken them if he thought he was coming back soon.

He's gone.

Coop isn't journeying to the center of the earth, but he's headed in that direction.

May tried to talk him out of it.

Coop listened carefully to all her reasons for not venturing into the Deep.

I could imagine him nodding, frowning, smiling, not saying anything, and totally ignoring all of her warnings.

And I could see why.

No one in the Community has ever been into the Deep.

Their information is based on rumors, urban myths, wild speculation, and a large dose of paranoia, based on exactly *one* face-to-face encounter.

Here's some of what they told me about the People of the Deep, or the "Pod," as the Community calls them.

Anywhere from a couple dozen to a thousand Pod live in the Deep (depending on which Community member you talk to).

They are satanists.

They are criminals.

They are drug addicts.

They are cannibals.

They are lepers.

They raise killer dogs to protect them and to chase down those who try to leave.

They speak a different language, but some of them know a little English.

Most of them cannot read or write.

They never take baths or showers.

They eat rats raw.

They never shave.

They can see in the dark.

They echolocate like bats.

They have lived in the Deep for generations.

They kidnap runaways from above as breeders to keep their gene pool healthy.

You cannot be a member of the Deep unless you were born there or kidnapped from above.

Their leader is a man named Lod, which stands for Lord of the Deep.

Lod paid the Community a visit, along with some of his people, the first week the Community arrived.

He ordered them to leave.

May convinced Lod that it was to the Pod's advantage to let them stay. In exchange for leaving them alone the Community would provide the Pod with food, supplies, whatever they needed. This way the Pod would not have to go up top.

This is what Posty was doing during the stops we made as he led me to the Community. He was making food and supply deposits in predetermined locations, dumping stuff into sealed garbage cans to keep the rats out.

After this initial meeting the Community never spoke to the Pod again.

The Pod left lists of the things they needed.

Posty and others said they'd see Pod members once in a while darting away, or hiding in the shadows waiting to pick up supplies, but they don't make contact with them.

Ever.

If Coop had gotten the same earful that I had just gotten,

and I'm sure he did, this is the question he would ask himself: If the Community has had virtually no contact with the Pod, how do they know they are satanic, foreign-tongued, drug-addicted, illiterate, dirty-rat-eating, bearded, cannibalistic, leprous, bat-like, criminal kidnappers?

Coop makes up his mind about people from his own personal experience.

Except for their initial meeting, the Community has had no personal experience with the Pod.

May and the others might as well have begged Coop to go look for the Pod.

He's been gone for almost a month.

No one knows if he's alive, lost, a Pod prisoner, or perfectly fine.

I asked if they would help me look for Coop.

This received an instantaneous and unanimous N-O.

They don't know where the Pod's compound is located.

They aren't supposed to look.

They told Coop not to leave.

He didn't listen.

He's on his own.

Subject closed.

NEXT SUBJECT

is the girl with the sunglasses.

Who doesn't speak and who might be deaf.

I say this because she finished her cake — I mean my cake — slowly, in complete silence, without looking up once as they debated her fate.

They came up with two solutions:

Turn her out on her own beneath.

Take her up with me and turn her out above.

They chose the second solution because they were afraid that if they turned her out beneath, she might just hang out on their doorstep. Or worse, find her way above and tell people where the Community is located.

They didn't care about what happened to the girl once she got up to the street.

What if she was deaf and mute?

What if she had never seen the sun or the moon or the sky?

What if she had the opposite of what I have? Agoraphobia. Fear of open spaces.

All they know about her is that she likes cake.

But the Community doesn't care about what-ifs.

Coop had seen right through them.

This is why he decided to head deeper.

He didn't find what he was looking for here.

I didn't either.

The question is, what am I going to do about it?

How can I find Coop if I don't even know where I am?

If they kicked me out without a guide, I'd probably wander around for weeks and starve to death before I found my way to the top. My bones would be . . .

"You just follow the fresh air . . ."

I jumped.

I switched the recorder off.

"How'd you get in here?"

"Through the door."

"You can talk."

"I can hear too, so keep your voice down. You'll wake the others. Coop told me all about you."

THE GIRL WITH THE SUNGLASSES

grabbed a towel off a hook on the wall and draped it over the lamp next to the bed.

She took her sunglasses off.

Her eyes were pale blue.

"You've seen Coop?"

"He used to talk into one of those," she said.

"What do you mean he used to?"

She reached into her pocket and pulled out a recorder identical to mine.

Smashed.

"It doesn't work anymore."

She handed the recorder to me.

"Where's Coop?"

"In the Deep."

"Is he okay?"

"I don't know."

COOP'S RECORDER WAS BROKEN

but the memory stick was intact.

I slipped the stick into my recorder and hit Play.

I left the Community this morning with dire warnings that I will never return. May's final words were: "No one who has gone into the Deep has ever returned from the Deep. This is the last mistake you'll ever make." She meant it sincerely, but I didn't take it to heart, as May doesn't know anyone who has ventured into the Deep . . .

I paused it.

"What's the matter?" the girl asked.

"It's Coop, but he doesn't sound like himself. He sounds . . . I don't know . . . more formal or something."

"He's writing a book. Or I should say, dictating a book."

"He told you that?"

"He said he was writing an episto . . . I can't remember how to pronounce it, but he's writing a story that reads like it's nonfiction."

"Epistolary novel."

"That's it. I suppose now he won't have to insert any fictional aspects. He's discovered enough to write a very interesting nonfiction book that can stand on its own. He said he was using some of the recordings you sent him for the book and from other people he's recorded over the past year."

His own *Journey to the Center of the Earth.*

Or *Dracula.*

The little snippet I just played sounded a lot like Jonathan Harker from *Dracula.* I remembered what Coop said in his very first recording to me. *You'll be able to transcribe all this into one of those journals you're always scribbling in. Epistolary. Remember that?*

Maybe Coop had gotten the recorder because he could not see to write in the dark.

"So I take it you can read," I said.

"Yes. And I can speak. And I'm not deaf. And my name is Katherine, but you can call me Kate."

She put out her pale hand.

I shook it.

I don't know what I was expecting, but the name kind of threw me. I guess I thought that someone who had lived underground her entire life would have a name like Root or something. Katherine was an open-meadow-with-wildflowers kind of name.

"Why didn't you say anything when everyone was talking about you?"

"Because there was nothing to say. I knew they wouldn't help me from the moment May took me in."

"They're going to take us both up to the top in the morning."

"I didn't come here to go up top."

"Then why did you come here?"

"To ask if they would help me free your brother from the Deep."

"Coop's a prisoner?"

"If he's still alive."

"What does that mean?"

"Keep your voice down. We can't talk here. I have to go. If you want to come with me, leave your pack. You can only take what you can carry in your pockets. They'll be here soon."

"Who?"

"The Pod."

THREE

THE DEEP

THE DOG'S NAME

was Bouncer.

A mutt.

About twenty pounds.

With smoky-gray fur and a docked tail vibrating madly upon seeing Kate.

She undid the rope, and Bouncer demonstrated how he got his name.

"Okay," I said. "We're outside. What's going on?"

I had to keep bobbing and weaving so Bouncer couldn't lick my face.

"I'll explain while I get ready." Kate handed me the flashlight I had given her from Coop's shelf.

She caught Bouncer in mid-bounce and flipped him onto his back. He didn't seem to mind. She pulled her sweatshirt off and put it on the dog. It was too big for him. He looked embarrassed.

"We'll have to make some alterations. Do you have a knife?"

I had a brand-new knife. I handed it to her.

She cut the sleeves off so Bouncer wouldn't stumble over them with his front paws.

"What are you doing?"

"Making a decoy."

She cut the sleeves into strips and used them to tie the sweatshirt around Bouncer's front legs and stomach.

"That should hold. We'll let him get used to it for a couple of minutes."

Bouncer started running around in circles getting used to it.

"I was shocked to see you arrive at the Community. Coop said that you had claustrophobia."

I was shocked that Coop had told her that he had a brother who had claustrophobia.

"He told me about the tunnel you and he dug. He said the collapse was all his fault, that he shouldn't have taken you down there."

"He did most of the digging. And I was nervous about the tunnel before it collapsed. And if it wasn't for Coop, I'd be dead. What's going on between you and Coop?"

Her pale skin flushed red.

She looked away.

That was all the answer I needed.

Coop had a girlfriend.

Or a girl who liked him a lot, which would not be a first.

I wondered if he felt the same way about her, which *would* be a first, unless I had missed one or two while he was gone.

Bouncer seemed to have gotten used to his ridiculous-looking costume.

He sat at Kate's feet panting.

"Go top and stay!"

Bouncer jumped up, did an airborne one-eighty, and vanished into the darkness.

"What's all that about?"

"Bouncer is one of our top dogs. We use them to find our way up from the Deep. I trained him."

"Then you've been to the top?"

She smiled and said dramatically in a pretty good imitation of May, "I have seen the sun and the moon and the sky."

I laughed.

I saw why Coop might like her.

She had the same weird sense of humor he did.

"So everything May and the others said about the Pod is wrong."

"Not everything." She looked at me for a moment. "I haven't even asked if you want to do this with me."

"Find Coop? That's why I came down here."

"I know, but you probably didn't expect all this."

"When you have a brother like Coop, you learn to expect the unexpected."

She waved the flashlight around. "I meant this," she said.

The beam barely penetrated the blackness.

"I'm not afraid of the dark."

"That's not what I mean. How'd you do on the way down here?"

"I was blindfolded."

Kate stared at me.

"I had a little problem when I squeezed through the entrance. After that I was okay."

"Before you decide to come with me, let me tell you what

you're in for. Pretty soon the dogs are going to show up here. Big dogs. Vicious dogs . . ."

"Killer dogs?"

"Not quite, but close enough. If they get you cornered and you try to run away, they'll draw blood. We call them Seekers. They don't get out much, which makes them all the more aggressive when they do get out. They get so excited during the chase they're hard to control."

"Who do they chase?"

"People who leave the Deep."

"You can't leave?"

"Not permanently, not alone, and not without Lod's permission. You can only leave if you have official Deep business beneath or on top. To make sure people return to the Deep we are always accompanied by a Shadow. Deep security people. They are there to protect the Pod and to keep an eye on them. If someone gets away, the Shadow is in as much trouble as the person who got away from them. But no one has ever gotten away."

"Never?"

An odd look crossed her face.

"No," she said. "And very few people have tried."

"What happens when they get caught?"

"I'll tell you later. Right now you have to decide whether you're going with me. By now Lod has discovered that I'm gone. He's coming with the Seekers and the Shadows. When they get here they are going to give the Community a rude awakening. They will question and intimidate them. Hopefully the Seekers will pick up my scent on Bouncer, assume that I'm headed to the top, and follow." She pointed the flashlight to a ledge of concrete about four feet above our heads. "There is enough space for us to hide up there, but it will be a tight fit."

Tight.

"It will probably take them fifteen minutes to search the Community and figure out I'm not here. When they continue to the top we'll drop down and backtrack along their route for a while, then we'll take a detour. This is where you might have a problem."

"What kind of problem?"

"A claustrophobic problem. The route we're taking is going to be hard for you. Maybe impossible. I'm smaller than you and it's hard for me. Lod and the Shadows could never squeeze through there."

Squeeze.

My chest tightened.

"Why can't we just go down the way they come up?"

"Time. The detour will save us hours."

"Hours? How long does it usually take to get to the Deep?"

"From here, if you hurry and know the way, twelve hours minimum. It will take Lod and the Shadows a couple of hours to reach the top and find Bouncer. Fourteen hours to get back to the Deep. Using the detour will give us a ten-hour lead, and we'll need every minute of it to get to the

Deep, free Coop, and head back up a different route. Coop is too big to fit through the detour."

That didn't sound good. Coop isn't that much bigger than I am. Or at least he wasn't when he left.

"Why don't we just go to the detour right now and start down?"

"Because I have to know how many Seekers and Shadows Lod has with him so I know how many he's left behind. If I know how many he has with him, and who they are, I'll know where Lod will station the others and how many are back at the compound. To get to the top we'll have to get around them."

"How do you know all this?"

"Because I'm one of them. I'm a Shadow."

KATE GAVE ME A LEG UP

I pulled her up to the ledge after me.

She was right.

It was tight.

I closed my eyes and concentrated on breathing.

Keep the panic down.

When I opened my eyes it was as dark as if they were closed.

Kate whispered.

"Coop told me that the only person who would help was a man named Taps, but when I got here I overheard one of them say that Taps had left for the holidays and wouldn't be back until after New Year's. If Coop is still alive, it will take at least two of us to get him out. There's another person who might help us, but he's old, and a little unreliable."

"What do you mea —"

"Shh . . . they're coming. Not another word until I say you can speak. And don't cough or sneeze."

A dog barked.

Then another.

They sounded far off, but within seconds they were there.

Panting. Sniffing. Pawing.

Lights dancing in the dark.

Heavy footsteps.

Out of breath.

Shouts.

Pounding.

Kate peering over the edge. Counting?

I hit Record.

"Open the door . . ."

"Settle down, Lod. We thought you might be coming."

"Where is she?"

"Gone.

"There's no need for rough stuff."

"Get that dog away from me . . ."

"I will decide what's needed and what isn't needed. We'll do whatever we want whenever we want. We have an agreement. A treaty. You violated the terms."

"We didn't violate any terms. It's not like we invited her here. She showed up on our doorstep on her own."

"Search the place. Get everybody out here."

"She's not in there, Lod."

"How long ago did she leave?"

"I don't know. I was the last to go to bed and that was a couple of hours ago."

"Did she leave alone?"

"Yes . . . well, except for her dog."

"Pat's gone too."

"Who's Pat?"

"A visitor I brought down tonight. He's the brother of one of our Community members."

"Which Community member?"

"He's not here."

"That's not what I asked."

"His name's Coop."

"The kid you sent to the Deep."

"We didn't send anyone to the Deep. We don't even know where you're located. He went exploring on his own, against our advice."

"He found us."

"How you deal with him is up to you. It's none of our business."

"He's one of yours. That makes it your business, and now it looks like his brother is with her."

"Like I said, Lod, we didn't even know she was from the Deep. She never said a word. We thought she was a mute."

"She can speak all right and often does. What were you going to do with her before she slipped away?"

"Turn her out, or take her up top and dump her."

"If she comes back here, I want you to hold her for me. And my dogs will know if she's been back here or not, so don't try to fool me. There will be repercussions."

"We'll hold her."

"Who is she?"

"None of your business!"

NONE OF YOUR BUSINESS

lay next to me perfectly still as the lights, voices, and barks faded away.

Five minutes passed.

Ten minutes.

Fifteen minutes.

Kate whispered, "Lod might have left a Shadow and a Seeker behind, but I think it's clear. I would have heard something by now if they were waiting. We'll have to do this all in the dark. No light until we get to the detour, where we can't be followed. I'm going to lower myself down first. When you follow, dangle from the ledge. It will be about a three-foot drop. I'll catch you if you fall. Sound carries for miles down here. We don't want the Community to hear us, or Lod."

Kate dropped without a sound.

I landed unevenly.

She stopped me from reeling over backward and held me in silence for a full minute, listening, then took my hand and led me away from our hiding place.

Not a sliver of light came from the door to the Community or anywhere else.

Utter dark.

Kate moved very slowly, quietly, without stumbling.

How was she able to see?

"How are you doing?" she whispered.

"I'm fine," I answered, but I wasn't.

The darkness was closing in on me like an avalanche of coal.

"You're hand is sweating," she said.

"I'm nervous."

"This is the easy part."

There was nothing easy about this.

"Can you see?" I asked.

"A little. But mostly I'm using touch and smell and air to find my way."

Air.

Breathe.

I took some deep breaths. It helped . . . a little.

I was clutching her hand like a vise.

I loosened my grip.

"What do you mean by air?"

"Temperature. Puffs of cool and warm air combined with smell. Don't worry . . . Coop didn't get the hang of it either, and he didn't have claustrophobia. Your hand is drier. You're not sweating as much."

She was right.

My hand felt less clammy.

And I was breathing easier.

But I still couldn't see anything except black.

"We're coming to some debris on the ground. You'll have to be very careful where you step. If you twist or sprain an ankle you won't be able to continue. Step lightly. Don't put weight on your foot until you're sure you're on solid ground. I'll slow down."

It was hard to believe we could move any slower without coming to a complete stop, but she managed it one slow step at a time.

Toe touch.

Test.

Adjust.

Ease the foot down.

Over . . .

. . . AND OVER

again.

"Shadows are chosen by the time they are two years old. We're picked based on our agility and reactions in absolute darkness. I know you think we're walking in the dark now, but there's actually a little bit of light here. Not enough for you to see, but my eyes pick it up. This is why I wore sunglasses inside the Community's compound. Sitting in that dim room was like sitting in a desert at high noon without a cloud in the sky with no shade. If I'd taken the glasses off, I would have been blinded . . . at least temporarily. From the time we can walk we're trained in a special room with a complicated maze and obstacle course. We're given tasks. Like finding a piece of candy or our favorite stuffed animal, and we're not let out until we complete the task."

"It sounds cruel," I said, feeling the ground for my next step.

"It's not as bad as you think," Kate said. "And becoming a Shadow gives you a lot more freedom than other members of the Pod. For the most part you can come and go as you please. Part of a Shadow's job is reconnaissance and exploration, which is how I came across Coop . . . starving, hopelessly lost, infected hand, over two weeks after he left the Community."

"Infected hand?"

"Terribly."

"You took him to the Pod?" I asked.

"No. He got caught. We got caught. Your brother didn't listen to me."

MAYBE I SHOULDN'T HAVE LISTENED TO KATE

either.

We started up what felt like a mountainside of loose rubble.

"Try not to disrupt the debris," Kate said. "If the Shadows come by here, they'll notice."

We couldn't hold hands on the rough terrain.

"Maybe we should use a little light," I suggested.

"I supposed we should."

Kate slipped a headlamp over her forehead and clicked it on. I did the same.

"What is this?"

We were standing on a mountain of red bricks, splintered wood, broken windows, rotting carpet, bathtubs, sinks, and several toilets.

"It used to be an apartment building," Kate said. "A hundred years ago."

The treacherous rubble pile was steeper than I thought.

"Won't the Seekers track us here when they find out we didn't go outside?" I asked.

"Is it snowing up top?" she asked.

"It was when I came down."

"Good. That will confuse them. They're going to find Bouncer sitting on the sidewalk. Did I put the sweatshirt on

114

him to keep him warm or to throw them off my track? Did I send Bouncer up top and take a different exit myself? They'll send the Seekers out a few blocks to see if they pick up my scent. New snow covers smells and will make that difficult. If we're lucky, they'll waste time checking out a couple other exits."

"That still doesn't answer my question," I said.

"Yes," Kate said. "Eventually they'll track us here, but they won't climb up the pile."

"Why?"

"I'll show you."

A BARKLESS DOG

A basenji.

Brown and white.

Pointed ears and snout.

Sweet-looking.

Silent.

I thought I might black out.

What had my heart pounding now was how Kate had retrieved the dog.

When we reached the top of the pile she got onto her back, put her arms above her head, and squirmed into a black hole the size of a small television set like she was being swallowed by a snake.

She seemed to be gone for a long time, but I'm sure it was only a few minutes.

She squirmed back out feet first.

Her arms still above her head.

Her right hand holding a rope.

On the other end of the rope was the dog.

Kate brushed sticky grime and spiderwebs from her face and hair.

She scratched the dog's ears with a filthy hand.

"We call her Enji. I used her because the breed doesn't bark. The Seekers would have heard her when they came by

116

here." She gave her another scratch on the head. "And I'm rather fond of her."

I didn't say anything.

"Is there a problem?" Kate asked.

The problem was that Kate had emerged from the serpent's mouth in the same position she had entered it, which meant that it was so tight inside she wasn't able to turn around.

"Is that the detour?"

"We'll talk about that in a minute," Kate said. "Right now I need your T-shirt if you're wearing one."

I was.

IT WAS SOPPING

with nervous sweat.

I was happy to strip out of it and felt sorry that Enji was going to have to wear it.

Kate said that she would send Enji back to the Deep the long way. The Seekers and Shadows would follow her. She took the T-shirt in one hand and Enji in the other and scrambled down the rubble pile like a mountain goat.

I guess she'd been taking it easy on me, which made me want to do better.

I shined the light down the hole.

I wasn't sure I could do that at all.

Kate climbed the pile almost as fast as she'd gone down.

She nodded at the hole.

"What do you think?"

"I don't know."

I was ashamed to admit it, but that was the truth.

I wasn't sure I could wiggle through that hole and survive.

"How long is it?"

"Long. It will take us at least two hours to get through it."

"Does it open up farther down?"

Kate shook her head.

I thought I might be sick.

"We have three choices," Kate said gently.

She took my hand.

I almost started crying.

She could not possibly have any idea of the overwhelming suffocating dread I was experiencing.

YET SHE WAS SO KIND

"We can go the long way," Kate said. "We'll get to the Deep hours before Lod and the Shadows return, but I'm not sure how long it will take us to get Coop out. I'd have to disable the security cameras. Then there is the problem of running into them on their way back."

"What's the second choice?" I asked.

"I can leave you here."

"But you said it would take two people to get Coop out."

"It will. I can't get him out. All I can do is distract everyone while the second person frees him."

"So, the second option is out," I said.

"Maybe," Kate said. "There's someone else who might help, but he's not in the best of shape physically, and I'm not sure he's up to the task mentally either. His mind wanders."

"You mentioned him earlier. Is he a member of the Pod?"

"No. He's a friend of mine. The Pod doesn't know about him."

"Why?"

"Because I never told them about him," Kate answered. "There's another problem with the second option. If you stay here, we would be forced to come back this way to pick you up."

"There's another way up to the top?"

"Yes, but I don't know where it is."

"Then how do you know there's another way up?"

"It's a long story. Right now we have to decide what to do."

"You didn't mention the third option," I said, looking back at the dark hole.

"I didn't think that was an option anymore."

WE BOTH KNEW

there was only one option.

I was going to have to get on my back, squeeze into the hole, and slither my way headfirst through spiderwebs, rat droppings, and slime.

"I have a thought," Kate said.

Anything would be better than what I was thinking.

"Do you still have your recorder?"

"Yeah."

"And Coop's recording?"

"Yeah."

"And earphones?"

Actually, my pockets were stuffed with things, including my journal, disposable cell, spare batteries, and other junk . . . but I saw what she was getting at. Well . . . I *heard* what she was getting at. I could barely *see* anything.

The idea was that if I listened to Coop's recording as I squirmed through the tunnel with a billion pounds of Manhattan on top of me, the sound of his voice might keep my mind off of where I was.

And the truth is that I want to hear your voice, and I hope that you still want to hear mine . . .

It might work.

If it didn't, I might hyperventilate until I passed out,

which happened on the first flight our family took after the Great Tunnel Disaster, wrecking our Christmas vacation.

I pushed the light button on my digital watch: 12:10 a.m.

"Merry Christmas," I said.

"All I want for Christmas is Coop," Kate said.

"Me too. Let's go see if he's under the tree."

Kate gave me her sunglasses.

"I don't think I'll need these."

"I have an extra pair. They'll prevent things from getting into your eyes."

Things, I thought. *What kind of things?*

I put them on and connected my earphones to the recorder.

"Once we're inside you'll have to push yourself with your legs and pull yourself with your hands. But be careful what you grab. I'll go slow."

"Go fast," I said. "I don't want to be in there any longer than I have to."

"Are you sure you want to do this?"

I put the earbuds in my ears.

Pushed Rewind.

Got on my back.

I HIT PLAY

as Kate's feet disappeared into the hole . . .

I didn't take it to heart, as May doesn't know anyone who
has ventured into the Deep . . .

It was damp.
My shoulders touched both sides of the tunnel.
My forehead scraped the top if I raised it too high.
Things caught in my hair and dropped on my face.
I tried to block out everything but Coop's voice.

. . . I have enough food for several weeks if I'm con-
servative. Mostly canned tuna. Water isn't a problem. There
is water everywhere below, and I have a filter. I guess
my biggest worry is not being able to find my way back.
It's easy to get disoriented down here. I have white chalk
to mark where I've been, which should help. I have three
flashlights, a handheld and two headlamps, plenty of
batteries.

My eyes have adjusted to the dark over the years, but
to acclimate them even further, I've been wearing shades
on top the past several months, even at night. I'm not sure
if this has helped. What I've found is that sight is not

nearly as important as touch, feel, smell, and hearing in the dark.

Community members all use flashlights and headlamps, but Taps told me that the People of the Deep, or the "Pod" as they're known, don't use artificial light at all . . .

Yes they do, I thought.

Coop probably knew this by now.

And a lot more about the Pod.

More than he wanted to know.

What I knew was that hearing his voice was working. Not 100 percent, but I was squirming forward, bumping into Kate's boots, and I hadn't gone catatonic.

Yet.

Taps drew me a rough map of the underground . . . at least the places he'd been, from what he could remember. He's been beneath longer than anyone in the Community. Or the Pod, so he says. When he was young he would go on "walkabouts" with no destination in mind. "Like them aborigine dudes from down under."

He was gone for more than a month one time and never backtracked or saw the same thing twice.

"Thought I might run into aborigines," he said. "Crazy, I knows, but stranger things have happened. Beneath is not a place. It's a country, where the sun don't shine and the birds don't sing. I calls it Echo Land, because all you hear is yourself and the past caving in on itself."

At the end of the second week I ran into one of these cave-ins . . .

Note to Pat: Meatloaf, you'll be happy to know that I bought a watch. Digital. Cheap. But it has a lot of buttons and whistles, or alarms. On top, time means everything. Beneath, it means nothing. When it mattered I didn't have one. Now that it doesn't matter I have one. Go figure. I actually bought it to determine where I am in the dark, or at least how far I've gone. I tested it above. It takes me about twenty minutes to walk a mile. Down here it probably takes a little longer because I have to climb over rubble and squeeze through openings. And of course it's dark down here. With this digital tape recorder and watch I've turned into a real geek . . .

When I hit the cave-in I thought my walkabout was over.

Half my tuna was gone, and I thought it might be time to head back to the Community. The bad news was that for the first time in my life I was sick of eating tuna. The good news was every time I gagged down a can the load in my pack got lighter.

I followed the impassable concrete, bricks, wood, dirt wall for two days, climbing into every nook and cranny only to find them dead-ending after a few feet. I began to wonder if Taps had steered me in the wrong direction. He and May and Posty ganged up on me before I left, trying one more time to stop me from leaving. They said that a walkabout wasn't safe anymore because of the Pod. Posty even offered to give me money to go back home, or if I didn't want to do that, he said he could get me a job at the library. Apparently he knows someone who works there. I turned him down. What they don't understand is that I have to do this. I've been heading this direction all my life.

I'm not looking for the Pod specifically, but if I bump into one of them, I'm going to make contact. When I was with the Community I abided by their rules. "Under no circumstances are you to initiate contact with members of the Pod." This was a little frustrating for me when I saw a Pod member lurking in the shadows as I made food and supply drops with Posty and Taps.

I'm on my own now. The rules don't apply.

But I haven't seen a sign of the Pod.

Coming and going as they do you'd think it would be easy to find them, but they cover their tracks well, just like the Community . . . better than the Community.

I decided to spend one more day, or night — there really is no day down here — looking for an opening, and that's when I discovered the fake chunk of concrete. It looked just like the other chunks, but it was made out of fiberglass and there was a handle on it.

I almost wept when I found it. I'm serious.

A wave of relief and exhaustion overcame me.

I slumped to the ground.

This is it.

As soon as I recover.

I'm going through.

The tunnel, or entryway, is about a hundred feet long, man-made, well used . . .

On the opposite end are a set of rickety wooden steps . . .

At the bottom is a river . . .

Not a stream . . .

An actual river with flowing water.

Maybe forty or fifty feet across.

I can't see the other side with my flashlight.

There's a dock with a large storage cabinet. Inside are old clothes . . . coveralls, coats, hats . . . ratty-looking with holes and a sour smell . . . and wigs and fake beards. Apparently the People of the Deep, or whoever the clothes and fake hair belongs to, disguise themselves . . .

Why?

There's a boat tied to the dock.

I'd like to report that the boat has been hollowed out with primitive tools by an ancient civilization, but . . .

It's made out of fiberglass . . .

There are cushions on the seats.

Mounted on the front is a searchlight.

On the back is a battery-operated motor.

Lying on the bottom is a fishing pole and a tackle box.

Underground fish?

Folded neatly on the benches are fresh clothes . . . clean clothes. The Pod must change into the dirty clothes when they go up top.

*   *   *

I'm looking at the map . . .

There's nothing about an underground river.

If Taps knew about the river, it would be on his map. He either didn't make it this far on his walkabout, lied about what he found, or I've gotten turned around and I'm lost.

Do I take the boat? If I take it, do I go down- or upriver? Do I strand the person who brought the boat? Or do I wait here for the person to show up? Stealing their boat is probably not the best introduction to the Pod.

I'll wait. I'll go fishing . . .

I caught a fish, but it cost me. I used the lure already tied to the line, threw it into the middle of the river, and immediately felt a sharp tug. I jerked the pole up and the line started playing out. I cranked the reel as fast as I could and landed the flopping two-pound fish on the dock. I'm not sure what kind of fish it was.

Silver . . .

Angry . . .

I didn't expect to catch a fish and had no way to cook it on the wooden dock. I let it go, which turned out to be more difficult than catching it. I got stabbed several times by its spiny fins and managed to imbed the treble hook in my palm. So much for my first fishing experience. But at least there's protein down here if I need it.

I'm thinking again about borrowing the boat, but I don't

129

because there's an unspoken law Beneath: Don't mess with people's things.

Still, I'm going to break this law . . . a little.

I borrow — take — some fishing line and a couple of small, rusty lures. If food becomes a problem, I can eat a fish, and I hope it tastes different than tuna.

I'll wait. If the boat owner doesn't show up, I'll go above and get my own boat. An inflatable.

Maybe even a fishing pole.

No wonder the Pod haven't been found . . . No one else has boats Beneath . . .

I just slept for six hours. I'm rested.

My head is a little clearer. Hungry. My hand hurts where the fish spines and hook jabbed me. The boat is still tied to the dock. I hate to backtrack and go up top to find a boat, of all things . . . That could take me weeks, but I don't have a choice. I can't steal their boat, and I can't sit on the dock indefinitely. Even if someone shows up, there's a good chance they won't take me with them, and it might not be a good idea to let them know that I've discovered their entrance . . .

"It gets a little tight up here," Kate said.

I paused the recorder.

If it got any tighter, I would have to tear my shoulders off to get through.

"You okay?"

"Yeah," I lied, and something fell into my mouth. I gagged it out, trying very hard not to think about what it was.

"What happened?"

"Nothing. Let's keep moving."

I switched the recorder back on.

Coop was out of breath . . .

I was on my way back up the stairs and caught something out of the corner of my eye . . .

A ledge. Carved into the rock on the right-hand side. Twenty feet above the river.

It was a stretch to get to it, and narrow.

I clung to the damp wall. Inched my way along in the pitch-dark.

My headlamp didn't do me any good with my face smashed against the rough wall.

The only thing that kept me going was knowing that if I fell, I would land in the river.

I might survive.

After a while the ledge got wider.

I found a steel cable bolted into the rock that allowed me to move faster. The cable led me to a three-foot-wide path with a sturdy rail along the riverside. And this is where I'm standing right now.

The river is far below.

I can hear it, but I can't see it.

The path is an incredible feat of engineering.

If it's the work of the Pod, it had to take them years to complete, hanging on the wall with chisels and picks, or maybe jackhammers.

Who knows what they have or how advanced they —

There's a light coming upriver.

The boat.

I just switched off my headlamp, and I'm watching the boat's searchlight swing back and forth across the water.

I can't see how many people are aboard, and they can't see me. I guess I'm heading in the right direction . . .

I don't know where I'm going.

But I've been headed there all my life.

KATE STOPPED

We were in another tight spot.

An earbud got scraped out of my ear, and I wondered how I was going to get it back in.

"Halfway," Kate said.

She sounded a *half* mile away, but I knew she was right there because I was touching the bottom of her slimy boot with my hand.

At least I hoped it was her boot.

"Are you still doing okay?" Kate asked.

I felt like I was clawing my way out of my own grave.

"Fine," I answered.

Another lie.

"You're going to make it," Kate said. "Going back would take as long as going forward."

Her boot pulled away.

I still hoped it was her boot.

I skinned my elbow getting the earbud back into my ear, then squirmed along after her.

ON THE PATH

there are signs of life.

Litter.

Footprints in the dust. Dog poop.

At least I think it's from dogs.

This must be an alternative route to the Deep. In the summer the river level must drop. Maybe there isn't enough water for the boat. Or boats . . . I'm sure there's more than one.

That means they have to haul supplies on their backs along this path. Unbelievable.

The searchlight disappears upriver quickly, and I'm back in the dark with my headlamp on. I'm happy I didn't take the boat now. Must be a Pod boat.

I've been on the path for more than an hour and a half, making good time. Five miles, maybe more. My left hand is swollen and throbbing. I took a couple of aspirin a few minutes ago and I hope that helps.

The path is descending, and I see a dim light in the distance growing brighter as I draw nearer . . .

There are steps carved into the rock on this end — no attempt to hide the path like there was on the other end. The steps lead to another dock — larger than the first, with seven boats moored to it.

Three old-fashioned lampposts light the area with flickering gas flames. The river flows out of a giant cavern. On either side are two cave-like openings. Both are lit with gas lamps attached to the walls.

Right or left?

As I decide, I look at my left hand in the dim light.

My fingers are swollen. I can't make a fist. My watchband is tight. I loosen the band.

I decide to take the left cave, but it's not really a cave. It's a tunnel carved out of solid rock. I can't tell if it's natural or man-made. If it's the latter, it must have been made with a tunnel boring machine, or TBM, which I read about in the library before I got below. I've been walking for several hours and there's still no end in sight. I've passed a dozen side tunnels, but I think it's best to stick to the main tunnel and find out what's here before I start any side trips. Unlike the river path, I haven't seen any signs of humans or dogs. But there are bats, thousands of them clinging to the ceiling, depositing mounds of slippery guano along on the tunnel floor . . .

The chalk I was using is worthless on these damp walls, so I took the time to sketch a rough map of my track so far. I'll add to it as I go along. The map's far from perfect, but it should be good enough to get me out of here if and when I have to leave. About an hour after I finished the map I heard rushing water. The tunnel had taken a sharp right turn back toward the river. Two hundred feet later I reached a dead end. There's a fifteen-foot gap across the river where the channel narrows. On the other side is an opening, but the only way to get there is along a single strand of steel cable . . .

I'm staring down at the frothing water, trying to figure out what to do. If I slip from the cable as I shimmy across, I'll be smashed against the rocky walls. My only other choice is to backtrack to the dock and take the other tunnel, losing several hours. I'm not in a race. I'm on a walkabout. What difference does a few hours make?

Everything.

I hate backtracking.

Even up top I always took different routes no matter how far out of the way they were. What's the point of going the same way twice?

I assume the cable is a shortcut to the other tunnel. It's unlikely there are two underground rivers running parallel to each other. The problem is my hand. The aspirin haven't helped. My legs are strong from tapping, but I'll need both hands to get across the cable. It's insane, but I'm going to give it a try . . .

I went through my backpack and found the fishing line I stole, a carabiner, and some rope.

I attached the carabiner to the cable and rigged a safety rope around my waist in case I slipped. I hooked the shoulder straps from my pack over the cable and tied the fishing line to it. No point in having thirty extra pounds weighing me down as I tried to pull myself across . . .

I'm glad I had the safety line. I slipped about three-quarters of the way across and dangled like a spider for about ten terrifying minutes. I guess I tied the rope a tiny bit too long — it was three inches from the end of my fingertips. I thought I was going to hang there with my head filling with blood until it burst. But I finally managed to snag the cable with my good hand, and after a Herculean effort, pulled myself up enough to hook my left arm over the cable.

I just landed on the other side and I'm out of breath . . . again. I don't know if it's because I'm nervous or because there isn't much oxygen down here, but I haven't experienced shortness of breath like this since I was hiking through the Canadian Rockies on my circuitous route to New York City.

There's a cable car hanging on this side, big enough to hold a few people or a large load of supplies. A rope is coiled up inside the car with a hook tied to the end.

I guess they toss it across the river and use it to pull themselves over.

The tunnel on this side has several branches. I can't tell which is the main branch. No gaslights on this side, so I'm back to using my headlamp.

I'm adding to my map. There's one tunnel on the left and two tunnels on the right about twenty feet down from the one on the left . . . They split into a Y . . .

I'm taking the left shaft for no other reason than it is slightly bigger than the other shaft.

It has a low ceiling. I have to keep my head down most of the way. A quarter mile down it opens into a big cavern with five openings. Three are directly in front of me, and two are on either side.

I'm taking the middle of the three in front, again because it appears a little bigger than the openings on either side.

I should mention here that all the tunnels I've passed appear to be long. I haven't been able to see the end of them with my brightest flashlight, but I suspect that some of these tunnels intersect with each other.

It's a maze down here, easy to get lost, easy to get confused.

Speaking of which . . .

I'm getting confused, or more accurately . . .

I'm getting anxious.

The rock walls are damp. They're cold to the touch, but I'm hot.

I've stripped down to my T-shirt. But I'm still sweating. My left hand still throbs. I'm still out of breath.

I'm not doing well.

This tunnel goes on forever. It's descending two thousand feet — maybe more.

My ears are popping. I'm thinking about turning around. I'm not sure if I have the strength to make the climb back up the tunnel.

What's wrong with me?

"What are you doing down here?"

"Who's there?"

"How many people are with you?"

"Where are you?"

"How many?"

"Just me."

"Then who were you talking to?"

"Myself. I'm talking into a tape recorder. Where are you?"

"Turn your headlamp off, turn the tape recorder off, and don't talk so loud. Sound carries for miles down here. People will hear you. You could be hurt."

I need to get this down.

In every detail so I don't forget our first face-to-face meeting . . .

After the voice in the dark — the first voice I'd heard in days — I heard footsteps, then nothing for a full minute until someone whispered . . .

"What are you doing down here?"

It was a young girl, by the sound of her voice.

I couldn't tell how far away she was.

My eyes hadn't adjusted to the dark yet.

"It's not safe."

"I know," I said. "I think I'm lost."

"That's not what I mean. Getting lost is the least of your worries. You shouldn't be down here at all. You've crossed the River Styx. No one has ever come back after crossing."

I laughed. The River Styx is a mythical river separating Earth from Hades written about by the poet John Milton in

Paradise Lost, and by Dante in *The Divine Comedy,* which wasn't at all funny.

The girl didn't think it was funny either.

"I'm serious. They know you're here. They're looking for you."

"Who's 'they'?"

"You know as well as I do. The Pod."

"How do you know?"

"Because I'm a member."

"Were you looking for me too?"

"Yes, and you're lucky I found you first."

"Why?"

"Because I can get you out of here before they find you."

"I don't want to get out of here."

"Then you're crazy."

"A little."

She turned on a small flashlight and pointed it at my swollen hand.

"And you're hurt," she said.

I saw her face for the first time.

The light was dim, but there was enough to see.

Black hair. Pale blue eyes. Petite. Wearing jeans and a pink sweatshirt.

She was beautiful.

She had a flashing Bluetooth in her left ear. I was curious about the Bluetooth, but I was more surprised about how I was feeling.

Tongue-tied. Anxious. Embarrassed.

Feelings I wasn't very familiar with.

I wasn't sure of the cause. It was either because I had given more credence to the Community's description of the Pod as demonic barbarians than I'd thought, and I was ashamed I had listened.

Or else there was something very special about this girl, something . . .

"What happened to your hand?" she asked.

"No big deal. It'll be fine."

"It's infected." She took a closer look. "Badly infected. It's not going to get better on its own." She flashed the light on my face. "You're sweating."

"It's hot down here."

"It's sixty-two degrees. It's always sixty-two degrees in the Deep. You have a fever. You need to go above and have your hand looked at. Get some antibiotics and then rejoin the Community. Never return . . . and never tell anyone what you saw down here."

"I haven't seen anything down here."

"Perfect answer," the girl said.

"You don't understand," I said. "I really haven't seen anything down here, and I'm not going above until I do. Why do you have a Bluetooth?"

"So I can hear the radio transmissions."

"How do radios work Beneath without towers?"

"That's not important. What's important is that you get out of here."

Something rubbed against my leg.

I looked down.

It was a little brown-and-white dog with a curled tail.

"What's his name?"

"Her name is Enji."

I squatted down and scratched her head with my good hand.

"You're starting to make me mad," the girl said.

"Why?"

"Because you're not listening to me. Because you don't believe you're in danger. Because I'm trying to save you and you're totally ignoring me."

"Sorry. I know your dog's name, but I don't know your name."

"Kate."

"Glad to meet you, Kate. I'm —"

"Coop," she said.

"How —"

"We watch the Community, but I knew about you long before you went Beneath. I've watched you tap above."

"Wait! You're the girl with the shades. I've seen you above on the street. I've tried to follow you!"

"I know," she said. "Why did you try to follow me?"

"I don't know. Curiosity? Why were you watching me?"

"Maybe I like tap dancing."

I laughed. "I didn't know the Pod ever went up top. I thought you —"

"Only a few of us are allowed up top. The Community couldn't possibly supply us with everything we need. And there are things we need and do that we don't want them, or anyone else, to know about."

"Like what?"

She didn't answer.

I tried another question. "You've watched me tapping?"

She looked away, embarrassed, and said, "Several times."

"Was I any good?"

"We don't have time for this. They'll be here any minute."

"What's the worst thing that could happen?"

She looked back at me.

"You could die."

THEY CAME

but they didn't catch up to us until we reached the gondola.

There wasn't time to throw the hook and pull ourselves across the Styx.

I didn't want to cross anyway.

Kate led me down a side tunnel, then pushed a large rock away from the wall.

"Stay inside. Don't move until you're certain it's safe."

I crawled inside, and she rolled the rock back into place.

There was barely enough room for me to sit up.

Kate was right about one thing.

My hand felt like it had been smashed by a sledgehammer.

I couldn't catch my breath.

The dogs arrived first.

They snarled and pawed at the rock.

"Here!" Kate shouted.

The dogs ran off. Seconds later I heard footsteps and saw flashes of light through the cracks around the rock.

"Did you see him?" someone asked.

"He was trying to get the gondola across," Kate answered.

"What did you do?"

"I pushed him into the river."

"You should have waited for us."

"It was easy. He was standing on the edge trying to throw the hook across. He didn't even know I was there. He dropped like a rock. Hit his head on the wall twice on the way down, slammed into that outcrop, then he disappeared beneath the surface. I think he was dead before he went under."

"You still should have waited, or at least radioed in. He might have hurt you."

"What would you have done?" Kate asked.

"Probably the same thing . . . Get Max on the radio. He and Susan are at the river cave. Tell them to keep an eye out for a floater."

"It's not likely they're going to find one. He was wearing a heavy backpack."

"Did you recognize him?"

"No."

"Not a member of the Community?"

"Definitely not. He was just a kid. Probably doing some urban exploring."

"How do you feel?"

"About pushing him into the river?"

"Yes."

"Happy," Kate said. "You don't need a weatherman to know which way the wind blows."

"That's my girl. Get the dogs. Call off the chase."

I MUST HAVE FALLEN ASLEEP

or passed out.

I opened my eyes.

Pitch-dark.

Just the sound of the Styx in the distance.

No voices.

No snarls.

Every bone in my body felt broken.

I pushed the rock with my good hand.

It didn't budge. It took both feet to move it.

Kate was a lot stronger than she looked. And a lot tougher by the harsh words she used describing my alleged death.

I crawled out and had to use the wall to get to my feet.

I stood in the dark wondering what I should do.

Drink water.

Eat.

I stumbled down the tunnel to the Styx hoping Kate had stashed my backpack.

I couldn't find it.

All I had on me was my headlamp, recorder, pocketknife, and watch.

I looked at the watch and thought it was broken. I couldn't have possibly been crammed in that hole for ten hours. But the digital seconds were clicking by one by one.

Ten hours of feverish oblivion.

There wasn't a morsel of food, but I did find an old empty can.

Pork and beans.

I punched a hole in the side with my knife, lowered it into the torrent with the hook and rope, and drank about a dozen cans of rusty water.

After that I felt a little better, but I still had major problems.

My hand. Kate was right — it wasn't going to get better on its own.

Food. It would take me at least two weeks to get back to the Community. I'd starve before I got there.

Light. My headlamp was working fine, but it wouldn't last. I couldn't make it back to the Community without light.

My thoughts were spinning.

There had to be a shorter way.

I must have been walking in circles before I found the opening.

It couldn't possibly take the Pod two weeks to get up top.

The men and women Kate was talking to at the river would have killed me.

Kate saved my life.

Kate watched me tap.

She's part of this.

But I'm not sure what role she plays.

If I go back now, I might never see her again.

I'll never discover what I've been looking for.

By the sound of it, Kate is way up in the Pod hierarchy.

Why did she risk her position — maybe her life — saving a complete stranger?

I want answers.

If I make it back to the Community, I might never get them.

"Why are you still here? Why are you still talking into that tape recorder?"

"Quit sneaking up on me!"

"I thought you'd be long gone by now. If you'd been listening instead of talking into that recorder, you would have heard me walking up."

"Did you hear what I was saying?"

"Some of it."

"Did you throw my pack into the river?"

"I had to make it look good. They snagged it downriver. They were disappointed you weren't attached to it."

"Everything I own was in that pack."

"Now everything you own is in the hands of the Pod. You can replace it all when you return to the Community."

"I'm not going back up to the Community. It took me weeks to get here. I'll starve."

"Enji will lead you back. I don't know how you got down here, but it will take you twelve hours to get back to the Community if you hurry. Maybe a bit longer in your condition."

"I'm staying."

"You're delirious. Didn't you overhear the conversation I had with the Pod?"

" 'You don't need a weatherman to know which way the wind blows.' "

"Not that part. The part where Lod couldn't care less about me pushing you into the Styx."

"I thought Lod was a myth."

"He's no myth."

"He seemed concerned about how you felt after pushing me into the river."

"He's protective of me."

"Why?"

"Because I'm his granddaughter."

"How long have you been down here?"

"I was born in the Deep."

"How many of you are there?"

"I don't know. Not all of us are in the Deep. We have people . . ."

I YANKED THE EARBUDS OUT

I had this irrational idea that I needed to breathe . . . through my ears.

The space had gotten impossibly tight.

With every ragged breath, my chest touched the rock overhead.

Kate moved faster, as if she could sense my panic.

"Can you hear me?"

"Yes."

"Breathe."

"I . . ."

"We're close to the end. Keep up. Fifty feet."

I MADE IT FORTY

"We're out. You're safe."

I heard the words, but they weren't clear.

They were too far away.

I was too far away.

Where was I?

Something wet touched my face.

I tried to sit up.

Something held me down by the shoulders.

"Not yet. You'll pass out again. Rest. Breathe."

The words sounded closer.

I was gasping.

I opened my eyes.

Kate was looking down at me.

She had a wet cloth.

She wiped my face.

Gently.

"How —"

"Don't talk. Save your breath. You almost made it. Ten feet short. I had to crawl out and come back in headfirst to get you. I thought you'd had a heart attack. You stopped breathing."

My chest hurt.

Maybe I did have a heart attack.

I closed my mouth and tried breathing through my nose.

It didn't work.

"You'll be all right in a few minutes."

A few minutes passed.

I was not all right.

I sat up and nearly blacked out.

Kate gave me a sip of water.

Finally I could breathe through my nose.

"Tell me we don't have to go back through there again."

Kate smiled. "I already told you: Coop is bigger than you. He'd never make it through."

"Good."

I took another sip of water.

"Thanks for pulling me out."

"It was the least I could do. I was the one who made you go in. And to be honest, I didn't think you'd make it as far as you did. That passage sometimes makes me panic, and I've been through it a dozen times."

"You were born in the Deep," I said. "Your grandfather is the Lord of the Deep."

"We have some time, and you should probably rest for a while."

"You should probably tell me what's going on."

SUBTERRANEAN HOMESICK BLUES

"What's that?"

"The title of a song from 1965, written by a musician named Bob Dylan."

"So?"

"Just listen. You're going to need your strength for the rest of the trip."

She took a drink of water and continued. "In the song there's a lyric that goes, 'You don't need a weatherman to know which way the wind blows.' In the late 1960s my grandfather was one of the cofounders of a group called the Weather Underground Organization, or WUO. They came to be known as the Weathermen, and they blew up government buildings and banks to protest the Vietnam War."

"Your grandfather was a terrorist?"

"Don't talk," Kate said. "Back then they were called radicals. The Weather Underground always warned people before the bombs went off so nobody would get hurt. Or at least that's what he told me . . ."

A look of doubt crossed her face. It was the same expression she had when I asked her if anyone had ever gotten away from the Deep.

She proceeded to give me the short history of the Pod . . .

Lod did not stand for Lord of the Deep . . . at least in the beginning.

His real name was Lawrence Oliver Dane.

In 1974 he led a group of thirteen faithful followers Beneath. He and a couple of the others were wanted for bank robbery, destruction of government property, kidnapping, murder, and several other lesser offenses, but they were all presumed dead, killed in an explosion and fire, and removed from the FBI's Most Wanted list in 1973.

Included among his followers were his wife, his son, and his son's wife (Kate's parents).

Lod had not gone into the Deep to hide. He had gone down the rabbit hole to establish a commune and continue the work of the Weather Underground, which was to destroy the US government.

The Weathermen who remained above were arrested, served their time, and most were now living relatively normal lives — their radicalism subdued or redirected.

But not Lod.

His life and the Pod's were anything but normal, and their radicalism was more extreme than it had been in the previous century.

Lod had gone Beneath with a plan . . .

"He had a map," Kate said. "He knew where he was going. He broke into a government building and discovered the plans and location of a top secret facility built during the Cold War in case of nuclear attack. It was built to last a hundred years and house up to five hundred people. It was provisioned, never used, and forgotten."

Early on there were problems.

Betrayals.

Fights.

Revolts.

After a few months people started wanting to leave.

Lawrence Oliver Dane became Lord of the Deep.

And no one who tried to escape ever made it to the top alive.

KATE HAD NO MEMORY OF HER PARENTS

They died when she was a couple of months old.

She was told that her parents had starved to death trying to reach the top.

Lod and her grandmother raised her.

"My grandmother died last year," Kate said. "Just before she passed she told me the truth about my parents' deaths. They did not die Beneath. They made it to the top, but my grandfather tracked them down. He murdered them, then took me back into the Deep.

"I didn't believe her . . . at first. She hated my grandfather. I thought she lied to spite him from beyond the grave. But I was wrong."

Kate took two sheets of crumpled paper out of her pocket. She handed them to me and positioned her headlamp so I could read them.

They were copies of two articles from the *New York Post* dated Christmas Day years earlier . . .

TWO DEAD IN DUMPSTER

The bodies of a man and a woman were found in a Dumpster outside Pallotta's Italian Grill yesterday.

"I was shocked," said Terry, a homeless man who refused to give his last name. He discovered the bodies while picking through the garbage. "When I flipped open the lid I didn't expect to find something like that. It was horrible . . . The worst thing I've ever seen in my life. And on Christmas Eve."

The homeless man notified the police immediately.

Detective Tia Muñoz said the victims were in their late twenties or early thirties. Both had black hair and blue eyes. The bodies had no identification. She requested that anyone with information about their identities, or the crime, contact her or the NYPD.

An anonymous donor has posted a reward of $2,500 for any information leading to the arrest and conviction of the perpetrator.

DUMPSTER
DEATH

There are still no leads in the tragic murder of a young man and woman found last week in the Dumpster outside Pallotta's Italian Grill.

Detective Tia Muñoz, in charge of the investigation, said that the unidentified couple died from multiple gunshot wounds, adding that the woman had been nursing before she was murdered.

"There's a child involved, so we might be dealing with a murder and kidnapping."

Fingerprinting yielded no information about their identity.

"Someone knows who these people are, or they have at least seen them and their child," Muñoz said. "The anonymous donor has increased the reward to $10,000. If you know anything about the victims, or their child, please contact me at the Midtown South Precinct."

THE ALLEY

I said.

"What?"

"The Community's postman discovered your parents," I answered. "We walked by the alley where they were found. He wouldn't go down it."

"The old man who works at the bank?"

"They call him Posty, but he goes by Terry Trueman, which apparently isn't his real name either."

"We keep a close eye on everyone in the Community, but I didn't know the old man was Terry Trueman." Kate thought a moment. "But I bet Lod knew. He knows everything about everybody."

"How?"

"The room," Kate answered.

"What room?"

"A place where only Lod and the Originals are allowed into."

"What's an Original?"

"The remaining eight men and women who have been in the Deep from the beginning. They would happily die for my grandfather. Not even I have been into the room. The rumor is that it's filled with computers and surveillance equipment. I think Lod has hacked into every camera in the city and has put up cameras of his own, and not just in New

York. Two Originals are in the room twenty-four-seven. And they all gather inside once a day to discuss Pod business and make plans."

"What kind of plans?'

Kate shook her head. "I don't know, but whatever they are, they're getting close to acting on them. He and the Originals have been busy the past couple of months . . . Coming and going up top, sometimes meeting several times a day for hours at a time, shutting down areas of the compound. I asked Lod about it. He said, 'Don't worry. You'll be safe.' I took this to mean that other members of the Pod will not be safe. I'm afraid. I think he's going to hurt people." She paused. "A lot of people."

"Did you tell Coop this?"

"I didn't get a chance to before we were caught. I didn't even get a chance to show him these newspaper articles."

I turned on my headlamp and took a closer look at the two sheets of paper.

"Where did you get these?"

THE LIBRARIAN

"The Deep has a librarian?"

"Are you kidding? We barely have books. And the ones we have are screened by the Originals. I was jealous of all the books the Community had, but over the years I've managed to read dozens of banished books with the help of the Librarian."

"Who is he? Or is the Librarian a she?"

"He," Kate answered. "And I don't know who he is. We've never spoken. I guess I better explain."

"I guess so."

Kate was thirteen years old when she discovered the Librarian. Or at least the first stack of books he had left for her. Along with a note:

Read these. Tell no one. They will take the books away.

You will be punished.

When you finish them I will lend you more books.

The Librarian

At first Kate thought it was a test.

Lod and the Originals were always testing the Shadows. She didn't touch the books.

But she didn't tell anyone about them either.

It took her four visits to the forgotten Murray Hill Reservoir beneath the New York Public Library before she picked up the first book and smuggled it back into the compound.

"I'd never been more frightened in my life," she said. "I read the book at night under my covers with a flashlight thinking that any second one of the Originals, or Lod, would burst into my room. I was the youngest person to ever become a Shadow, and there were . . . there still are . . . a lot of people who want me to fail. I bypassed a dozen people wanting the coveted position, including some of the Originals' family members. I could have been sent to the mush room for reading a forbidden book."

"What's the mush room?"

"You don't want to know."

Actually, I did want to know, but I let the question go and asked another.

"What was the first book?"

"*Lord of the Flies* by William Golding."

"The Librarian jumped right into it," I said. "What did you think of the book?"

"Subversive propaganda," Kate said. "You see, I told myself that I was going to play along with him by reading the books . . . but my real goal was to find out how he got into the Deep. With the exception of my detour, there are only two other ways into the Deep that I know about. And both of them have surveillance cameras, which are monitored around the clock. If I could catch an intruder and discover an unknown entrance, all doubts about my becoming a Shadow would vanish."

"If you were watching Coop on surveillance cameras, why didn't you stop him before he found the opening? You must have been watching him for days."

"We wanted to see if he could find it. We thought he'd give up."

"Coop never gives up."

"I've noticed," Kate said. "After a couple of days we thought for sure he would head back where he came from. By the time he was through we were hardly paying attention to him. He'd missed the rock a hundred times. No one was close when he slipped through and reached the river."

"You didn't know he was from the Community?"

Kate shook her head. "Our only option in the dark is to use infrared cameras, so all we can see are thermal images. No details. If I'd known it was Coop, I would have gone up and warned him off immediately."

"Not that he would have listened to you," I said.

"That's another one of his annoying traits."

I looked at my watch. "I'm feeling better. Shouldn't we get moving?"

"We still have some time."

"I thought we were trying to get as far in front of Lod as we could."

"We are, but there are other ways of increasing our distance than rushing to the compound. I have a way that might slow Lod down, but it has to be timed just right. I also have to get into the compound without anyone being suspicious of me. If they are, I won't be able to sneak you in and we'll have no hope of getting Coop out."

Kate read a book a night.

Sometimes two.

Her plan to find out who the Librarian was and how he was entering the Deep did not change.

But the books she read changed her.

Word by word.

Idea by idea.

Novels. Philosophy. Religion. Politics. Geography. History. Science. Art . . .

"I continued looking for the Librarian," she explained. "Sometimes spending the entire night hidden away waiting for him to pick up the books I dropped off. But I never saw him. I never heard him. All I would find was a new stack of books.

"I put our best Seekers on him. These dogs can track a single mouse for miles. But they never picked up his scent. It was almost as if the books were taken and replaced with new books by magic, but of course I knew they weren't.

"After a couple of years I stopped looking for him. I realized that if I caught him, there would be no more books. The books had become more important than proving myself as a Shadow. I thought I was using the books to catch him, but it turned out that he had used the books to catch me . . ."

AND THAT'S WHEN HE APPEARED

Kate walked up to drop off the books she'd read and there he was.

Sitting on a boulder.

Reading a book.

He didn't look up.

At first she thought he didn't know she was there.

He turned a page and kept reading.

Then another page.

And another . . .

Kate waited.

Finally he slipped in a bookmark and closed the book.

He looked up at Kate. "I dislike stopping in the middle of a chapter, don't you?"

"Yes," Kate said, barely able to find her voice.

"Have you enjoyed the books I've left?"

"Most of them."

"I didn't expect you to like all of them."

"Who are you?"

"A friend."

"It's not safe for you down here."

"I'm perfectly safe down here. I've been down here as long as your grandfather."

"How do you know about my grandfather?"

"I know everything about the Pod."

"Have you met my grandfather?"

"A long time ago."

"What's your name?"

"That's no longer important. I'm just a simple librarian now."

There was nothing simple about the Librarian.

Kate wasn't even sure he was a real person.

"What do you mean?" I asked.

HE MIGHT BE A GHOST

Kate answered quietly, looking away.

I understood why she was looking away.

Our escape. Coop's life. Depended on someone, some-*thing*, that might not exist.

"A ghost?"

"I'm not sure. I don't know what he is. All I know is that I've tried to follow him a dozen times and every time I do, he turns a corner and vanishes."

"Poof," I said.

"More or less," Kate agreed.

"And this is who we are depending on to get us out of here?"

"It's a long shot, I know."

Impossible is more like it, I thought. "What's he look like?"

"Old. He wears a tattered suit and tie. Thick, black-framed glasses. Gray beard. He smokes a pipe."

"How old is he?"

"Late seventies . . . eighties. I don't know. But for his age, he moves incredibly well."

"And he can disappear into thin air," I added.

"I know it sounds crazy."

"Does he know you're trying to get Coop out?"

"I'm not sure."

"All right. I'll put it another way. How do we find him so he can show us how to get out of here?"

"I don't find him," Kate said. "He finds me. At first I only saw him at the reservoir, but then he started popping up in the Deep, Beneath, and above."

"You saw him up top?"

Kate nodded. "A few times, but above we never spoke. I'd pass him walking down the street. Or see him watching me. He knows how the Pod operates. We work in teams up top. There is always a second Shadow within sight for security in case there's trouble."

I wanted to ask her what kind of trouble, but I was more troubled about Coop and how we were going to get him out of the Deep.

"Let me get this straight. We're relying on an old man . . . or ghost . . . who sometimes appears and sometimes doesn't, who can apparently vanish into thin air, who has no idea that we are trying to get out of here, and who may not know how to get out of here himself?"

"He knows how to get out of here," Kate said. "The books he's left for me are from the New York Public Library. And I wouldn't be so sure he doesn't know we're trying to get out of here. He could be watching us right now, listening to this conversation. Just before he gave me these articles he told me that I was leaving the Pod."

"How could he know that?"

"When he said it, I had no intention of leaving. In fact, I was still thinking about turning him in."

"But then you discovered your grandmother was telling the truth," I said. "The articles were the proof."

Kate nodded. "But here's what's strange. Look at the bottom of the pages."

I held them under my headlamp.

There was a time stamp on the bottom of both articles.

They were printed twelve years earlier, long before the Librarian began lending Kate books.

"Don't ask," Kate said. "Because I don't know the answer. All I know is that he always shows up when I need him. Somehow he knew all of this was going to happen. He'll help us if he can."

"And if he can't, or if he doesn't want to?"

Kate stood. "It's time to go."

"What are we going to do?"

"We're going to save Coop, but first I need to lie to my grandfather. At the right place."

THE RIGHT PLACE

was the path above the River Styx.

Kate jogged along the dark narrow ledge as if it were as wide and bright as a well-lit street.

I walked along behind, clutching the rusty railing, wondering if my claustrophobia had been replaced by vertigo.

When I finally caught up to her she was wearing the flashing Bluetooth Coop had mentioned.

"Another Pod rule," she said. "Shadows are not allowed to turn their radios off. Ever. I suspect that Lod and the Originals have special transmitters in the radios and use them to track us. I've had my radio off for more than twenty-four hours. I'm about ready to turn it on."

"Why?"

"Because I want him to know exactly where I am. I want to continue the argument I started with him three days ago."

"You confronted him about murdering your parents?"

"Are you kidding? If he knew I knew about that, he'd probably murder me. I'm talking about the argument I started when he caught us. He accused me of trying to get Coop out of the Deep. He accused me of trying to run away with him."

"Weren't you?"

"Of course, but if I admitted that, I'd be locked up like Coop. I insisted that I was bringing Coop in, not taking him above. I acted outraged that Lod could even think for a minute that I would leave the Deep, especially with someone from above. I didn't talk to him for two days . . . then I turned my radio off and disappeared."

"Poof," I said.

Kate smiled and took a very small radio out of her pocket. "I'm going to turn this on and put it on speaker. You might want to record the conversation for Coop. It will make an interesting addition for Coop's project if we get out of here alive."

She turned the radio on.

I HIT RECORD

"Where are you?"

"You know exactly where I am. Where are you?"

"Up top looking for you. You turned your radio off. You helped that kid escape. You broke our law, Kate."

"I stopped another topsider from getting into the Deep. And I proved that our security is weak."

"What are you talking about?"

"You walked right past me."

"Impossible!"

"At the Community. I was there watching you. I sent the kid up top with Bouncer, then I waited. There were eight of you. You were after me, not Coop's brother. You didn't even know he was Beneath, but I knew. How long do you think he would have hung around the Community waiting for Coop to show up? He wouldn't have. He's claustrophobic. He wanted out of there. He was going to get in touch with the authorities. I told him that Coop headed to Mexico with a girl he met from the Deep. That he wasn't coming back, that —"

"You listen to me . . ."

"No, Lod. You listen to me! A couple of days ago, according to you, that fictitious girl was me. I'm the one who found Coop and pushed him into the river, yet you accused me of trying to run off with him. I could have gone up top with his brother and

172

you would have never found me. But where am I? I'm headed to the compound, which you've left virtually unguarded, chasing someone who's not running. There is no one in the Pod more loyal to you than me. No one! This has got to stop right now, or I am going to leave."

This was followed by a very long silence. When Lod spoke he sounded like a completely different person.

"This is not how I wanted to spend Christmas. I don't want you to leave, Kate."

"Like you ever cared about Christmas, Lod. If you want me to stay, make me an Original along with two other Shadows of your choosing. You need to bring some young blood into the decision-making process. That's the best present you could give to the Pod for Christmas."

"We've talked about that."

"The time for talk is over."

"I hear you. I think it's time. But what about this boy . . . Coop's brother?"

"That's up to you. If you want to track and grab him, that's fine with me, but I don't think he's ever coming back down here. He doesn't know anything, and he's afraid of the dark. Like I said, I told him that his brother was on his way to Mexico. He's either on his way home or headed south to find his brother."

"I'll send a couple of Shadows and Seekers after him just in case."

"What?"

"I said I'll send a couple of —"

"*You're breaking up. That's another thing we need to fix. Our communication system is terrible. I don't know if you can hear me or not.*"

"*I can hear you . . .*"

"*If you can hear this, I'm heading down to the compound. I'll see you when you get there.*"

"*I'll be down in a few hours . . .*

"*I hate this thing. We've got to get this —*"

Kate reached up above her and pulled what appeared to be an antenna out of the wall and threw it into the River Styx.

KATE HAD A BIG SMILE ON HER FACE

"What was that?"

"*That* was beautiful," Kate answered. "What my grandfather just did was give me carte blanche when I get to the compound. He all but promised that I was going to become an Original. This means I'll be able to move freely through the compound with no interference. No one questions the Originals, and in our culture I'm pretty sure this will also apply to a potential Original. There are two Shadows left in the compound; the others are with Lod. Both of them are going to be very respectful because they know that with just one negative word from me to my grandfather, their chances of becoming Originals are zero."

"Are you saying they'd allow you to let Coop go?"

"No, but I might have enough clout to call a meeting, which would allow you to let him out."

"What's to stop them from coming after us?"

"Nothing. As soon as they know Coop is out they are going to try to run us down." She pointed to where she had torn out the antenna. "But I just took out all of their radio communication and cameras. They go out all the time, so no one will be suspicious. Lod won't know we're gone, or be able to coordinate the hunt until he gets back to the compound.

But the two Shadows that are there are good, and they're going to be highly motivated when they figure out I betrayed the Pod."

She started walking along the path again and looked back at me. "Are you doing okay?"

"I'm not afraid of the dark."

"I know."

"And I'm fine."

I actually was fine.

Considering where we were.

And what we were about to do.

FOUR

THE POD

WE TOOK THE RIGHT TUNNEL

Coop had taken the left.

Kate said that it was lucky he had.

"If he'd taken the right tunnel, he would have run into Lod before I found him."

I imagined Coop gushing through a narrow opening and being gaffed by a Shadow like a dead fish.

"You think Coop is okay?"

"Pretty sure. When I left he was in the infirmary. His hand was getting better. I've kept Lod and the Originals pretty busy since we got caught. We're not far away and they're going to be watching for me. You're going to need to turn your headlamp off and stay at least twenty or thirty feet behind me. If you hear me talking to someone, then veer off into the nearest tunnel and find someplace to hide. I'll come back and find you when I can. If I make it all the way to the entrance, I'll turn around and blink my headlamp twice. There will be a tunnel on your left. Go down it and wait for me."

"What if someone comes along?"

"Trust me. No one will go down that tunnel."

We had walked by at least twenty side tunnels.

"This place is honeycombed with tunnels. What if I go down the wrong one?"

"The tunnel you're going down doesn't smell anything like honey. It's our sewer egress. Not even the Seekers venture there."

"Nice," I said.

"About fifty feet down," Kate continued, "there's an air shaft with a fan. Don't worry, the air shaft is huge . . . nothing like my detour. Crawl inside and you should be able to escape the worst of the stench. But you might want to hold your breath until you reach it. It could be a long time before I can get to you. Don't worry, I'll be there."

YOU DON'T NEED A WEATHERMAN TO KNOW

how the wind burns your eyes.

By the time I reached the shaft it felt like mine were melting out of their sockets.

Kate forgot to mention that part.

But she was right about the fan.

It was like being in a wind tunnel.

I lay on my back, eyes watering, catching my breath.

I smelled bacon.

I looked at my watch.

Someone, somewhere, was cooking Christmas breakfast.

To take my mind off my hunger, and to save my ears from the roaring fan, I put the earbuds back in and hit Rewind, then Play.

Kate was speaking . . .

"Not all of us are in the Deep. We have people above."

"What do you mean?"

"We don't have time for this. You have to leave here, now."

"What about you?"

"What about me?"

"Why did you watch me tap?"

"It was amusing."

"It was more than that. Why are you helping me?"

This was followed by dead silence.

For a moment I thought the recording had ended.

But then Kate answered.

Quietly.

Softly.

"I don't know. There was something about you."

This was followed by another pause.

Then a voice that I knew was Coop's, but it didn't sound like him.

Nervous.

Stuttering.

Breathless.

As though if he didn't get the words out quickly, they would not come out at all.

"I know this sounds strange . . . bizarre . . . crazy . . . but I think I've been headed toward the Deep my whole life . . . looking for something . . . something important . . . something that will change my life . . . I didn't walk down here . . . I was pulled. The reason I started tapping was to keep my feet moving when I didn't know where to go."

Another silence.

Longer than the first.

I imagined the look of shock and derision on Kate's face.

And Coop's embarrassment at her response.

But I was wrong.

Kate said . . .

"Maybe I've been waiting too."

"Then you know that I'm not leaving without you."

"They'll come after us."

"Then we better get going . . ."

The recording ended.

Then sometime later . . .

Dogs howling.

Men shouting.

"I can't believe you'd run off with a topsider."

"I can't believe that you think I would run off with a top-sider. That's insulting!"

"What were you doing with him, then?"

"I was checking our security, like always, and ran across his trail. Obviously he survived the Styx. I was trying to grab him before he stumbled into the compound. I can't believe you'd accuse me of betrayal. I don't even know this kid. A few hours ago I tried to kill him."

"Maybe."

"What do you mean 'maybe'? I've had all of this I'm going to take! If you're going to treat me like this, I'm gone, Lod. I'm not going to take any more of this unwarranted abuse."

"What's that in his hand?"

"It's a broken flashlight. What? You think this kid's carrying a gun? Throw it away."

The sound of rushing air.

CRACK

That was the end of the recording, as Coop's recorder, aka the broken flashlight, smashed against the rocks.

I transcribed everything into my journal to pass the time.

It wasn't easy with the fan blowing and the smell of bacon churning my stomach.

Where's Kate?

Did Lod and the Originals believe her story?

Did they grab her as soon as she walked into the compound?

Was Coop in the mush room?

Was Coop alive?

HOURS

later Kate crawled into the shaft.

"I was worried. Where've you been?"

"It took me longer to slip back out than I expected. I forgot about Christmas breakfast. It's one of the compound traditions."

"I smelled it. Did you happen to bring leftovers?"

Kate smiled. "Sorry. I'll find you something to eat when we get to my quarters. The breakfast may have lost us some time, but it's also going to help us. Everyone wakes up early and we have this communal feast. Afterward, people go back to their quarters to celebrate the holiday with families or friends. This is usually followed by a long nap. No work on Christmas for most of the Pod. There won't be many people wandering around the compound. You should be able to find your way out easily."

"What about you?"

"I'll be distracting the Guards and the Shadows. I'll meet you and Coop as soon as I can get away."

"How is Coop?"

"He's shocked that you're down here."

"You talked to him?"

Kate nodded. "He's still in the infirmary, but his hand's a lot better. I relieved the guy guarding him so he could get some breakfast. We got here just in time. Lod was going to move him to the mush room tomorrow."

"What's the mush room?" I asked again.

"It's not really a room. It's an area . . . a very big area. It's how we make our money. We grow mushrooms and truffles and sell them up top. Everyone except the Shadows work on the mushroom farm. Three months on, three months off. It's unpleasant work. Pod members who fall out of favor are put down there permanently, or until Lod decides to let them back up. The Originals decided to make Coop a permanent laborer."

"Who runs it?"

"Lod's in charge, but I don't know who runs the day-to-day operation. People from above, I assume, or maybe Originals who even I don't know. Lod is the only person who knows all the pieces and how they fit together."

"How do they get the mushrooms above?"

"I don't know that either. But they aren't brought up through the compound."

"So, there's an exit there."

"There has to be," Kate said. "We sell mushrooms all over the world. But if you're thinking that we can use that exit, you can forget it. The Guards down there make the Shadows look like angels. They carry rifles and Tasers. And they have dogs that *will* kill people. Lod parades the Guards through the compound a couple of times a year, allegedly to meet with the Originals, but I think the real reason is to remind us what will happen if we betray him. I think Lod used the

Guards to hunt down my parents. I just hope he doesn't send them after us along with the Shadows."

The idea of terrible mushroom men creeped me out.

"What's the plan?"

"First I need to get you into the compound."

"How?"

"The same way you and Coop are going to leave."

KATE POINTED AT THE FAN

"I'm going to switch it off, but just for a second. You'll need to crawl past the blades quickly. The fan's monitored in the control room. If it's off too long, an alarm sounds and this place will be filled with Seekers and Shadows."

"What is this place?"

"Sewage treatment plant. The treated sewage is piped down to the mushrooms and used as fertilizer along with the garbage the Community brings us."

Treated or not, I was never going to eat another mushroom as long as I lived.

"Are you coming with me?"

"I can't. The Interrupt switch is only on this side. Even if I could turn it back on from the other side, I still couldn't go with you. I walked out the front door. If I don't return the same way, people will get suspicious. Crawl down to the first turn and wait. And be careful. You don't want to get sucked into the blades. I'll come and get you when I can and lead you to my quarters. Ready?"

I got down on my stomach and crawled as close as I dared to the swirling blades, surprised that I didn't have even a twitch of claustrophobia. After the detour the small space felt cavernous.

I looked back at Kate and nodded.

She reached up and flipped a breaker.

The fan did not come to an immediate stop.

The eye-watering stench returned.

I glanced back at Kate again.

Her hand was on the switch.

She looked nervous.

I started through before the fan came to a complete stop.

My feet barely cleared the blades before they started again.

I crawled on my hands and knees as fast as I could.

Turned right.

Took shelter against the wall.

I was in an air duct.

The smell of bacon was so strong I could taste it.

Kate had said that Coop was shocked I was here.

I smiled in the pitch-dark.

My brother was alive.

A BEAM OF LIGHT

bobbed toward me in the darkness.

I hoped it was attached to Kate.

It was.

She whispered, "No talking. Sound carries. Pay attention. Right. Left. Right. Follow me."

I did.

The air duct was . . .

darktightsqueezewiggleinsidecrawldown

. . . all the sensations that usually caused me to shut down.

My knees hurt.

My hands, scraped and bloody.

I was hungry.

Tired.

But not afraid.

Poof!

My claustrophobia had vanished.

Right. Left. Right.

"Turn your headlamp off," Kate whispered.

We crawled toward a dim rectangle of light.

It was a grate, hinged from the top.

She pushed it open.

Stuck her head through.

Looked both ways.

Flipped onto her back.

Did a backward somersault.

Now, face-to-face, I saw she had slipped on her sunglasses. She whispered, "Don't worry, you won't have to try that. I'll help you down headfirst."

If I *tried that*, I would be wedged in the vent forever.

She wiggled through the opening and disappeared.

I scooted forward.

She was standing in a dimly lit, narrow hallway made out of cement.

"I'll break your fall," she said.

"You better not try," I said. "Stand clear."

My exit wasn't as graceful as Kate's, but I managed to get down without breaking anything, including Kate.

"Do you really need sunglasses?"

"Shadows always wear shades. It keeps our eyes accustomed to the dark. If you see someone in the compound with sunglasses, it's a Shadow."

I glanced down the dim hallway. "Are there surveillance cameras here?"

"Yes, but they haven't worked for months. The only camera that still works inside the compound is the one covering the entrance. I wasn't kidding when I told Lod that our security is weak. And this is another reason why I'm suspicious that he and the Originals are getting ready to do something.

Maintenance used to be a high priority and a constant problem, but this past year they've let a lot of things slide. I think Lod is getting ready to abandon the Deep."

"Why?"

"I wish I knew."

I was getting a little nervous standing in a long hallway with nowhere to hide if someone happened to come along.

It must have showed.

"You're right," Kate said. "We should get moving."

It was a maze. Everything looked exactly the same. After about the fifth turn I stopped.

"What's the matter?" Kate asked.

"I'm already lost. How am I going to find my way back to the vent?"

"It's not as complicated as it seems. I drew a map for Coop. And he's pretty good at navigating underground."

"Have you forgotten how long it took him to get to the Deep?"

Kate smiled. "It's a really good map. All *you* need to remember is how to get to the fan."

I had to think about it for a second.

"Left. Right. Left."

"Perfect."

Kate pointed to a square of light about fifty feet in front of us.

"That's the door to the stairs. No one uses them. On the off chance someone does, we'll hear them long before we see them. The steps are metal. We'll go through the door to the nearest floor and find somewhere to hide until they pass."

"How many floors are there?"

"Including this one, thirteen that we have access to."

"What do you mean by *access*?"

"We have three elevators. The middle one has a key that allows it to go deeper. Lod has the only key. That's how he gets to the mush rooms. I have no idea how many floors are beneath us, or what's there."

WE TOOK OFF OUR SHOES

so they didn't clank on the metal steps.

When we reached the fifth floor we heard someone coming down.

Fast.

Kate grabbed my hand and pulled me through a doorway.

Another cement hallway.

Carpeted.

With numbered doors.

We ducked into 526 on the right-hand side.

Kate took her shades off and put her eye to the peephole.

"What is this place?"

"Living quarters," she answered with her eye still to the hole. "Apartments. No one lives on this side. There's no view."

Without taking her eye away she reached down and flipped a switch.

It was more like a cement cell than an apartment.

No windows.

Carpeted like the hallway.

Kitchenette.

No furniture.

Bathroom with a shower, toilet, and sink.

One bedroom.

No bed.

I wandered back out.

"We're clear," Kate said.

I followed her into the hallway.

She opened the stairway door and listened.

We sprinted up to the thirteenth floor.

There were several doors on the right-hand side, but only one door on the left, halfway down the hallway.

"Lod's lair," Kate said.

1300

was the number on the door.

Kate pulled out a lanyard from under her collar with a magnetic card attached to it.

"I've lived here my whole life," she said, swiping the card and opening the door. "I never thought I'd leave."

I might have felt the same way if my quarters were like Lod's.

It wasn't an apartment.

It was a penthouse.

Beautifully furnished.

Immaculately clean.

With a panoramic view of the compound through a window running the length of the room.

"None of this furniture came from a Dumpster," I said.

"Nothing in the compound comes from Dumpsters."

"What about the food and supply drops the Community makes?"

"It's a ruse," Kate answered. "Lod set it up so they'd think we were barbarians. He didn't want them trying to find us to see what we have here. We throw the stuff away, except the organic material for the sewer plant."

The Pod complex made the Community's circular room look like a kid's fort slammed together in a backyard.

There were two other towers. One on the right. One on the left.

Both of them were one floor short of the middle tower we were in.

Glass elevator shafts ran from the plaza to the top of each.

"Make yourself at home," Kate said. "The kitchen's over there." She pointed to a door. "And you can step up to the window and look out. It's mirrored two-way glass. No one can see in."

There was a spotting scope on a tripod next to the window.

I walked over and looked down.

Everything could be seen from Lod's lair.

There was a central plaza between the three towers with a huge swimming pool in the middle of it. Tables had been set up around the pool, where they had just served Christmas breakfast.

The only person in the plaza now was a man standing by a small door between the right and left towers.

"Guard," Kate said, joining me. "They work four-hour shifts. They're armed, but they've never pulled their pistols from their holsters as far as I know."

"Where's Coop?"

She pointed. "Left tower. Bottom floor. There are two sky bridges connecting the towers. One on the seventh floor and one on the third floor. Take the one on the third floor, then use the stairs. The infirmary is midway down the hall on the right side. He's in examination room number two, handcuffed to the bed. The key to the cuffs is in the nurse's desk, which you'll see when you walk in. Top right-hand drawer." She gave me her keycard. "You'll need this to get into the infirmary and into the examination room where Coop is."

"You said there was someone guarding the infirmary."

"Mike," Kate said. "I'll swing by and invite him to the meeting. He's a Shadow wannabe. He'll come. He wasn't happy about standing outside the infirmary guarding a handcuffed prisoner locked inside on Christmas Day."

"When do we leave?"

"I'll go down to the plaza in a few minutes. I told everyone about the meeting at the breakfast. As soon as they see me they'll start wandering down. Not everyone is going to show, but they'll be watching from their windows and balconies. This will give you and Coop a good chance of reaching the vent without being seen." She pointed at the spotting scope. "Keep an eye on me. I'll take my sunglasses off when I think it's okay for you to get Coop."

She handed me two pairs of sunglasses.

"What are these for?"

"A disguise," she answered. "Not a very good one, but the only people who wear sunglasses are Shadows. The Pod tends to avoid Shadows, since we keep an eye on them, as well as an eye out for intruders. If you happen to run into someone, just walk by purposefully, like you know where you're going and what you're doing. Chances are they won't say anything to you. Shadows make people nervous. They tend not to make eye contact with us."

"How many people are down here?"

"Well over a hundred in the compound and another dozen or so in the mush rooms. Then there are people up top who work for us, although I doubt they know much about us. Lod and the Originals are the only people who know exactly how many. Unless you're a Shadow, a Guard, or an Original, people keep to themselves. They are afraid to ask questions because that draws attention to them."

I put the shades in my pocket.

"Do I have time to get something to eat?" I asked.

Kate led me into a kitchen with cherry cabinets, granite counters, and stainless-steel appliances.

She opened the refrigerator.

It was stuffed with food.

"Wow!"

"We don't eat out of Dumpsters."

"I noticed you ate the cake."

"I have a thing for chocolate, and I watched their cook dump the ingredients out of a sealed cake-mix box. I figured it wasn't tainted."

"Where does all this stuff come from?"

"The commissary. Aside from food we can get almost anything we want except televisions, radios, computers, most newspapers, most books . . . Or 'Conduits of Corruption,' as Lod and the Originals call them. The store has all the food you'd find in a regular grocery above, and it's restocked a couple of times a week. A catalog is printed out once a month with furniture, appliances, and other goods. You pick out what you want and it arrives in a week or two. And it's all free.

"I guess when they first came down here it was pretty utilitarian. Canned and powdered food. Simple furniture. Nuclear bomb shelter decor. By the time I came along the mushroom farm was producing and things had changed."

I made two bologna-and-cheese sandwiches and washed them down with a quart of organic orange juice.

Then I mixed up some tuna and mayo and made Coop a couple of sandwiches to go.

I didn't believe he was sick of tuna.

THE CHRISTMAS BREAKFAST

tables began to fill with men and women.

I don't know what I was expecting.

Troglodytes — ancient cave dwellers.

Morlocks, from H. G. Wells' novel *The Time Machine* — another favorite of Coop's — who feasted on the flesh of the Eloi who lived above.

Some had long hair; some had short hair.

Some had beards; some were clean-shaven.

They were well dressed.

Perhaps because it was Christmas.

They were clean.

Their skin was a little paler than most people's.

Other than this, the Pod looked absolutely normal.

Kate seemed relaxed around them.

Smiling.

Chatting.

Some wore shades.

Shadows.

They had no idea what she was about to do.

She looked around to see if anyone else was coming.

KATE SLIPPED HER SHADES OFF

I slipped mine on.

I left Lod's lair.

The thirteenth floor was no problem.

The stairs down to the third floor were no problem.

The sky bridge wasn't what I expected.

It was open, long, and narrow.

I was totally exposed.

No more than a hundred feet from the gathering.

I wanted to sprint across but knew that would attract attention, so I *walked purposefully, like I knew where I was going and what I was doing.*

About halfway through my purposeful walk I glanced down at the plaza to see if anyone was watching me.

They weren't.

They were all staring at the glass elevator shaft in the center tower.

The car was descending.

It disappeared beneath the bottom floor.

It stopped.

No one spoke.

No one took their eyes off the shaft.

The car came back up into view.

The door slid open.

Three men stepped out.

And two dogs.

Rottweilers.

"I thought Christmas breakfast would be over by now," the man in the middle said loudly.

I recognized his voice.

The Lord of the Deep.

He had a gray beard and long gray hair tied in a braided ponytail.

He was big.

The two men flanking him were bigger.

They were not wearing shades.

Their dogs were not chained.

The men were not clean.

They wore shoulder holsters with pistols.

Mush room Guards.

Morlocks.

They looked hungry.

So did their dogs.

"Where are the others?" Kate asked.

"Looking for that kid."

That kid was standing on a sky bridge, out in the open, and with his mouth hanging open in complete shock.

Lod had taken a shortcut of his own and picked up a couple of friends who looked like they had eaten their children for Christmas breakfast and then thrown the bones to their dogs.

"Like I told you," Kate said, matching Lod's bluster. "That kid is long gone. Headed south or headed home."

"Not according to the Seekers. He never made it to the top. He's still Beneath."

"They've been wrong before," Kate said. "But we should certainly make sure."

She stood and put her shades back on.

"That's why I brought reinforcements," Lod said.

"Good."

"When we catch him we'll take both brothers down to the mush rooms."

"Even better," Kate said.

Lod pointed at the people sitting at the tables. "What's all this about?"

"Just an informal gathering to talk about security and Pod business."

"Aren't you getting a little ahead of yourself? You're not an Original."

"Yet," Kate said, smiling.

Lod smiled back.

"We'll talk about that after we make sure the other kid isn't down here."

"Fine. What about the radios?"

"They're still out. I sent a couple of people back down to check the antennas."

"It's going to be difficult to coordinate a search with communications down."

"We'll manage."

"Then I guess we better get started."

The kid on the bridge got started too.

Or restarted.

I shouldn't have stopped to eavesdrop.

But if I hadn't, Coop and I might have died.

OVER THE BRIDGE

Down the hall.
    Down the stairs.
    To the infirmary.
    Swipe card.
    Top right-hand drawer.
    Key.
    Examination room number two.
    Idiotic grin.
    "Hey, Meatloaf."
    Coop.
    "Hey."
    His hair was longer.
    He hadn't shaved.
    He wore a skimpy hospital gown.
    "I can't believe you came down here."
I handed him the tuna sandwiches and the key. "Merry Christmas."
    "It couldn't have been easy for you."
    He unwrapped a sandwich one-handed.
    "It was worth it."
    Tears rolled down my brother's cheeks.
    Mine too.
    "Let's get out of here."

"My clothes are in the closet."

I started to get them.

"Someone's coming. Under the bed!"

I slid under.

The door opened.

Boots.

Rottweiler paws.

"I told you he was secure," Kate said. "Putting Mike on the door is redundant. We'll need him for the search."

Lod walked over and shook the cuffs.

"What are you going to do with me?" Coop asked.

"We didn't invite you down here. You came of your own accord. You'll be staying. And so will your brother."

Coop laughed. "My brother would never come down here. He's a claustrophobe. He could no sooner come down here than you could fly."

"He made it to the Community."

"I don't know how that happened, but trust me . . . Once he got there he was on his knees begging them to take him back up top."

"We'll find out about that," Lod said. "I see your hand's better. When we get back, these two gentlemen will be escorting you to your new home . . . Do I smell tuna fish?"

"Christmas breakfast," Coop said.

"You didn't eat much of it."

"Since you only feed me once a day I've learned to ration my food."

"Good practice," Lod said. "Do you like mushrooms?"

"Not really."

"Too bad."

The boots and paws left the room.

The door closed.

"Wait," Coop whispered.

I waited.

When I finally slid out, Coop was sitting on the bed eating his tuna sandwich.

"You were always good at making tuna salad."

"You said you were sick of tuna."

"That's because I was eating it three times a day for weeks without mayo. The mayo would have gone bad in my pack."

He unlocked his cuffs.

I got his clothes.

He finished his sandwich while he dressed.

"Do you have any idea how crazy these people are?"

"They're not all crazy," Coop said. "But Lod and most of the Originals are way out there."

"Most?"

"The woman in charge of the infirmary is one of the Originals, and she's relatively normal."

"And she spilled her guts to you."

Coop grinned. "Most of the contents. Enough for me to figure out that there are big changes coming to the Deep."

"Did she tell you about the two Morlocks with the Rottweilers?"

"Yep," Coop answered. "Mush room Guards, bad dudes . . . and there are more than two of them. In fact, I think that's one of the reasons she was so forthcoming with information. She knew I was being sent down there and that whatever she told me would never resurface."

"And you understand that we're in like . . . mortal . . . danger here?"

"Kate filled me in this morning."

"She told you about Lod killing her parents?"

"Horrible."

"And the Librarian?"

"Yeah."

"What do you think about that?"

"The books he got had to come from somewhere. I hope we can find him . . . or that he finds us."

"If we don't find him, we're sunk."

He looked in the closet and pulled out his tap shoes. "Remember when you got me these?"

"Christmas."

"Someday I'm going to get you something you want for Christmas."

"You already did."

"Huh?"

"I wanted my brother back for Christmas."

"Some present," Coop said, stuffing a tap shoe into each of his back pockets.

LEFT, RIGHT, LEFT

I said.

We were standing under the vent.

Coop had led us there.

From memory.

Without one wrong turn.

He had eaten Kate's map so they wouldn't find it on him. He said it wasn't nearly as good as the tuna sandwich.

"Left. Right. Left," Coop repeated. "Couldn't be simpler than that. We'll have to do it backward."

"What do you mean?"

"You'll have to go in feet first so you can pull me up. I'm not as small as Kate, nor as agile. I want to latch the grate behind us. I don't know how long it's going to take Kate to get to the fan, or how long it will take for them to discover I'm gone. When they do, they're going to search every nook and cranny of the compound."

We put our headlamps on.

Coop cupped his hands and boosted me up.

I grabbed a pipe attached to the ceiling and walked up the wall to the grate.

I crabbed my way inside, flipped over, then reached down and pulled Coop up.

Left.

Right.

We stopped.

The conduit before the final turn was five times as big as the one we'd just squirmed through. We were able to sit facing each other.

Knees up.

"So, what do you think of her?" Coop asked.

"Kate?"

"Duh."

"Smart. Beautiful. Articulate. Tough. Great actress. Contortionist. Everything you'd want in a girl. I listened to your recordings."

"Kate told me."

"Do you really think she's the reason you've been driven Beneath all these years?"

"It could be. I know it sounds crazy."

"No," I said. "It sounds like Coop. What do you think the chances are of us getting out of here?"

"Excellent."

"That sounds like Coop too," I said. "Do you know something I don't know?"

"I might."

"Care to share?"

"I find it hard to believe that I could have been looking for this all my life, only to find it, then die."

"Or become a mushroom picker for the rest of your life," I added.

"Right. But you know what I mean. And I have to admit

that last night, Christmas Eve, I wasn't feeling my optimistic self. I hadn't seen Kate since I got caught. I was handcuffed to the bed. No one knew where I was. The woman treating my hand said they were taking me to the mush room the day after Christmas.

"Then this morning Kate walks into my room, tells me that you're down here and that we're leaving sometime after breakfast.

"And now my hopelessly claustrophobic brother is sitting with me in a cramped vent, thousands of feet beneath the surface, grinning, as if he doesn't have a care in the world."

I had a lot of cares.

My grin could have just as easily been a grimace.

But that was impossible with Coop sitting inches away from me.

"How'd you get over your claustrophobia?"

"Immersion. I think."

"Kate couldn't have done this alone."

"She seems pretty resourceful."

"I guess I better tell you something before we start running for our lives," Coop said. "The hardest thing I ever had to do was to walk away from you after the tunnel collapse. I didn't want to. But I felt it was the only way I could protect you. I thought this was my journey alone. I had no right to endanger you by inviting you along. I may have been wrong about that, because here you are. I'm sorry, Pat. I should have at least kept you in the loop."

COOP LOOP

I said.

Coop laughed.

That's when the fan started to wind down.

Kate was clearly relieved to see us, but all she said before she switched the fan back on was "Hold your breath."

We stumbled out of the sewer tunnel.

Eyes watering.

Gagging.

Kate led us to another tunnel to catch our breath and regain our sight.

"I thought I was dead when Lod insisted on checking on you in the infirmary." She looked at me. "You were under the bed."

I nodded.

"Why did you take so long to leave?"

"I was on the bridge when Lod came out of the elevator. I listened for a few minutes. I got to the infirmary just before you came in. Sorry."

"You have nothing to be sorry about. If Coop had been gone when Lod walked in, the Rotts would have been on you before you reached the basement. That's about the only good luck we've had."

"What's the matter?" Coop asked.

"My grandfather. He has almost the entire compound out looking for Pat. He's calling it the Christmas Drill. But what he's really trying to do is prove me wrong. I embarrassed him publicly."

She looked at her watch.

"And in about forty-five minutes, when they bring your dinner to the infirmary, he's going to be proven right."

"With the radios out it will take them a while to let him know," Coop said.

Kate shook her head. "The radios are back up. Not only that, he's making everyone work in teams just like we do up top. I teamed up with Mike. The Originals are in the control room tracking us right now . . . especially me."

"You don't have your Bluetooth," I said.

"I left it with Mike along with my radio. Turns out he has a weak stomach. When I started down the sewer tunnel he lost his Christmas breakfast. A lot of people do the first time. I told him that Lod would never make him a Shadow if he found out. He's waiting up ahead with Enji."

"What are we going to do about him?" Coop said.

"He won't come to the sewer tunnel looking for me, but he's not going to wait where he is forever either. He'll call in and say that we got separated or something. I don't want to hurt him, but if I have to . . ."

Coop reached into his pocket and pulled out his hand-cuffs. "These didn't hurt and they kept me from wandering around."

"Those will do nicely."

Coop offered to give her a hand with Mike, but she turned him down, saying that Shadows were well trained.

The diminutive Kate walked off with the cuffs.

"You've spent more time with her than I have," Coop said. "What do you think she meant by that?"

"I think she meant that Mike wouldn't be a problem for her, and neither would we if she decided to kick our butts."

KATE RETURNED

with two radios clipped to her belt and Enji at her heels.

"What's to stop Mike from yelling his head off for help?" Coop asked.

"Pride, and his ambition to become a Shadow. After I got him handcuffed to a pipe I told him that I could cover more ground on my own. If he started hollering, the Shadows would come running and Lod would want to know how a girl that he outweighed by eighty pounds managed to hand-cuff him. His Shadow dream would be over. I told him that I would be back for him."

"What now?" I asked.

"I'll check in with Lod, then we go for a boat ride."

She put her Bluetooth in and turned on the speaker.

"Lod?"

"Go ahead."

"Mike and I are with Enji. She's picked up something, but it comes and goes. Can't tell if it's Coop's old scent or some-one else's, but Enji's going crazy."

"Dogs are onto something here too, but there's no clear trail."

"I don't believe it's his brother, but I think you're right about having an intruder down here. Maybe Coop wasn't alone."

"I'll have our friends from the mush rooms have a chat with him about that when we get back to the compound."

Kate let out a harsh laugh.

It was chilling how she could switch personalities so easily.

"We're going to head up and meet the Shadows coming down. Enji has a better nose than the other Seekers. We'll see if she can pick up something they missed."

"Are you going to take your *secret* shortcut?"

Kate hesitated. "You know about that, huh?"

"Of course."

"We're going to take it. I thought it might be a good way of testing Mike. See how he does."

"If he makes it through that rubble, I'll make him a Shadow."

"He's grinning."

"Keep in touch."

"We will."

Kate took the Bluetooth out.

"He knew about the detour," I said.

"They must have discovered it when they backtracked from up top. They probably sent a Seeker through and had it wait at the other end. Which means Lod is toying with me. He knows more than he's saying, but he doesn't know as much as he thinks." She unclipped the radios, attached them to Enji's collar, then spoke very deliberately to the little dog. "Slow. Shortcut. Up top. Avoid."

Enji trotted off into the darkness.

"If she goes too fast, Lod will figure out that she's carrying the radios. *Avoid* means that if she encounters people up ahead she's to take another tunnel, or hide until they pass. It will buy us a little time . . . but not much. Turn your headlamps off and follow my light at a distance. Look for potential hiding places. If I run into someone, stop and hide. I'll backtrack and find you."

Kate backtracked three times.

It seemed that the Deep was overrun with People of the Deep.

None were Shadows.

None had radios.

All three were perplexed over why Lod was having a drill on Christmas Day.

One man was hopelessly lost.

He nearly wept with relief when Kate told him how to get back to the compound.

WE REACHED THE RIVER STYX

through a small but long side tunnel, crawling single file, with Kate in the lead.

"I was afraid of that," Kate said.

She was in front of us peering over the lip of the opening. The water sounded fast.

"Afraid of what?" Coop asked.

"The water level fluctuates. The canoe is twenty feet below."

I hadn't seen any canoes on my way through the Deep.

Coop hadn't mentioned canoes in his recordings.

"We can climb down," Kate continued. "But it's slippery. I've fallen in more than once." Suddenly she switched her headlamp off.

"Back up! Quick! Quick!"

Coop and I backed up like crawfish.

A light flashed across the opening.

"They know," Kate said.

"They know where we are?" I asked, scooting farther back. As if that would help.

"Not yet," Kate said. "But that was Lod's boat that went by. He wouldn't be on the river unless he's discovered that Enji is carrying the radios, or that Coop is not in the infirmary. He's heading downriver to the upper entrance and there's another boat coming behind him."

Another flash lightened the tunnel, then went away.

"Does Lod know about your canoe?" Coop asked.

"If he knew, he'd be tied up below waiting for us!" Kate snapped.

This was the first time I heard her speak harshly . . . at least to us.

"Sorry," she said immediately. "I'm just . . . well . . . I mean . . . The River Styx has turned into the River of No Return. I've lived in the Deep my whole life. I have friends here . . . or I did."

She was crying.

I think.

I couldn't see the soles of Coop's boots.

"No light," Kate continued. "No talking. Voices carry over the water. And I'm sure there are Shadows posted along the path above the river watching and listening. I'll climb down and throw a rope up to you."

I decided it wasn't a good time to tell her about our swimming problem.

Coop didn't mention it either.

Knowing Coop, he may have forgotten that he didn't know how to swim.

This turned out to be true.

Three minutes later, when I slipped on the rocks and fell into the river, Coop dove in to save me.

Which is when he remembered that he couldn't.

Kate dove in to save both of us.

Me first, since I had been drowning the longest.

Coop second.

There was nothing silent about the mishap.

As we held on to the side of the canoe hacking and spluttering, Kate snapped at us for the second time.

Without apology.

The only good thing about the incident was that she was sure there were no Shadows nearby.

"If there had been," Kate said, "the Pod would be all over us right now."

THE CANOE

was as black as the river.

Kate paddled in front.

Coop paddled in back.

I sat in between.

Shivering.

Trying not to cough.

Wondering what kind of deadly bacteria I had just sucked into my lungs.

I probably wasn't going to live long enough to find out.

Searchlights appeared up- and downriver.

The canoe was matte black inside and out, and virtually invisible against the rock wall. Kate handled it expertly, keeping it close to the wall as if she'd done it hundreds of times before.

"Kate!"

The Lord of the Deep's megaphoned shout ricocheted off the rocky walls like bullets.

This did not cause even the slightest hiccup in Kate's rhythmic paddling.

"We know everything!"

Kate continued paddling.

"The Pod are everywhere!"

Slicing through the water.

Left.

Left.

"All of the exits are guarded!"

"You cannot get away!"

Right.

Right.

Smoothly.

"I'm willing to put this all behind us! Just bring me those boys!"

Left.

Left.

Steadily.

This is when I realized how strong Kate was.

If I were her, I would be shouting back.

You murdered my parents!

You kidnapped me!

You lied to me!

Right.

Right.

Silently.

With each quiet stroke she was destroying the man who destroyed her parents.

"Kate!"

The searchlight in front of us was getting brighter.

"I know you can hear me!"

Kate brought the canoe to a stop.

"I know you're frightened!"

She reached out and pulled the canoe snug against the rocks.

"There is nothing to be afraid of if you do the right thing!"

She motioned for us to lie flat.

I stretched back.

Coop stretched forward.

Face-to-face.

A searchlight passed over the canoe well above the waterline.

A woman was talking to Lod on the radio.

I switched the recorder on.

Coop grinned.

"... *the other one was inside the compound too. Seekers tracked him up to your floor outside your door. We didn't go inside, of course, but we're assuming* . . ."

"*He was* inside *the compound?*"

"*Definitely.*"

"*How could that happen?*"

"*We're trying to figure that out.*"

"*Maybe they're still inside.*"

"*We're still searching, but I doubt it. We just found Mike.*"

"*And?*"

"*Kate slapped the kid's cuffs on him. The only way those cuffs could have* . . ."

Lod's boat motored out of hearing distance.

Kate whispered, "The dock is around the bend. Shadows and Seekers will be waiting. The river's wide there. Normally they can't see the other side, but they'll have searchlights. I need to switch places with you, Pat. I'm going take us past there on my own."

"Where does this river go?" Coop asked as we switched.

"It empties into the Hudson, but you can't get there from here. The final quarter mile is completely underwater. We'll take a side tunnel before we get there. I suspect Lod has dropped Shadows in some of them. I just hope they aren't in the passage we're taking."

As we switched places it occurred to me that we weren't rescuing Kate.

She was rescuing us.

But she might not have left if Coop hadn't gone down.

SHADOWS ON THE DOCK

Two of them.

A third on the path above.

Searchlights dancing.

Kate back-paddled just out of reach of the beams.

Watching.

Waiting.

If there was a pattern, I couldn't see it.

Kate paddled forward, then stopped, just as two beams swept past the bow and the stern.

Close.

I could hear her breathing.

Stop.

Go.

Back.

Forward.

I thought the dance would never end.

But it did.

Kate let out a long sigh as the dock disappeared behind us into the gloom.

KATE STOPPED

and we climbed onto an outcrop barely big enough for the three of us to stand on.

"You can use your headlamps now."

She pushed the canoe out into the current and watched it float away.

"Where are we?" I asked.

"Beneath the reservoir. Sometimes the Librarian waits for me right here as if he knows I'm coming. I was hoping that would be the case today."

"Let's go find him," Coop said.

"You don't find the Librarian," Kate said. "He finds you."

She led us around a large boulder. On the other side was an opening to yet another tunnel.

"How'd you find this place?" I asked.

"I've been exploring the Deep since I was ten," Kate answered. "I just hope Lod doesn't know about it like he knew about the detour we took."

It was a tight squeeze, but once inside we could stand.

Bats hung from the ceiling.

"They're hibernating," Kate said. "Try not to disturb them . . . they'll fly out into the cold and die. I've found some of my best passages by following bats in the spring when they wake up."

But the *rats* were not hibernating.

Hundreds of little shiny eyes darted around as we made our way up the steep path to the reservoir to find a ghost.

Then the eyes vanished.

"That's strange," Kate said, stopping.

"What," Coop said.

"The rats. They're gone."

Kate started walking again, cautiously.

We stepped into a very large cavern.

Three lanterns burned.

One of them was on a flat rock.

Next to the lantern was a small stack of books.

No Librarian.

"Something's wrong," Kate said.

SOMETHING GROWLED

A Rottweiler stepped out from the shadows.

Forty feet away.

Snarling.

"Game's over."

A mush room Guard stepped out and stood next to the dog.

He raised his radio to his mouth.

"Got 'em."

"Where?" Lod asked.

"Reservoir."

"All three?"

"Yep."

"Don't hurt Kate."

"What about the boys?"

"They're yours. We're about a half hour out."

He clipped the radio to his belt. "You heard him," he said.

Kate flipped her headlamp off.

"If you run, I'll send the dog . . . but not after you. The young boy first. He'll be dead in five seconds. You know our dogs, Kate. They aren't weak like your dogs."

"You're going to kill them anyway," Kate said.

"We all die, but I can think of a lot better ways of going than being torn apart by a Rott."

Kate took Coop and me by the arms and pulled us close to her.

"I can think of a worse way to go," she said. "His name's Lod."

She took a step toward the dog and pulled us with her.

The Rott snarled.

The man reached down and grabbed the dog's collar. "What do you think you're doing?" he shouted.

"I'm betting that if you send your dog, he won't be able to control himself. He'll kill all three of us. Then you get to explain that to my grandfather. We're going to turn around and walk out of here. Together."

The man reached for his gun.

An explosion ripped through the cavern.

The dog flew into the air and hit the ground.

Dead.

"Drop the gun, cowboy."

The Guard looked around wildly.

A second shot peppered his boots.

"The game is just beginning. Next one's in your chest."

The mushroom man dropped his gun.

"The Taser and the radio."

He dropped the Taser and the radio.

"Who are you?"

"Step away from the weapons."

The mushroom man stepped back with his hands up.

An old man stepped into the light.

A ghost with a shotgun.

The Librarian.

"Sorry about the dog," he said. "Turn around."

The Guard turned around.

The Librarian picked up the Taser.

THE LIBRARIAN

watched the Guard convulsing.

"I would have rather shot him than his dog," he said. "But I couldn't control the dog."

"Will he be okay?" Coop asked.

"You mean will he live? He'll be out for a while, and when he comes to he'll be sore, but he'll live. His kind always lives. We have to leave. Follow me."

He walked over and picked up the stack of books.

All three of us hesitated.

I don't know what Kate and Coop were thinking, but I was still shocked.

Killer dog.

Dog killed.

Guard twitching.

My ears were still ringing from the shotgun blasts.

"I know you," Coop said.

"Right. We met in the library. I told you about the under —"

"I know you too!" I said. "I talked to you at the post office. You said you didn't know Coop . . . I gave you five bucks. 'Merry friggin' Christmas.'"

"Merry Christmas to you too," the man said. "Now let's get out of here. I need to get you above and on your way.

You've stirred the wasp's nest. In a couple of hours they're going to be swarming the streets looking for you. I'll explain everything when we get to the library."

His bad leg did not slow him down.

Nor did the darkness.

He had an old flashlight that he had to bang once in a while to keep lit, but I don't think he needed it.

He was better at negotiating the labyrinth than Kate.

And quicker.

We made a final turn and came to a solid rock wall.

He looked at Kate. "Did you ever get this far?"

"I think so," she answered.

"And you thought it was a dead end."

Kate nodded.

"That's the problem with the Pod. You're always looking straight ahead or down. You rarely look up."

He pointed his dim flashlight up a narrow shaft.

Just above his head was an iron rung.

Three feet above the first was a second.

One hundred and two altogether.

At the top was a metal trapdoor locked with a padlock.

He unlocked it with a key hanging around his neck and pushed the door open.

When we were through he closed the door, flipped the hasp over the staple, slipped the padlock through, and locked it.

"That'll hold 'em . . . for a while."

"You think they're going to find this place?" Coop asked.

"Kate couldn't."

"She wasn't looking hard enough. Lod won't stop looking until he does find it. That's guaranteed." He looked at Kate. "We're in a forgotten subbasement below the library. I'm going to turn the lights on so these boys don't fall all over themselves. You might want to put on your shades."

Kate slipped them on.

The lights weren't very bright, but even I was blinking and squinting.

Our boots echoed down the long concrete hallway.

I glanced at Coop.

"Don't even think about it," I said.

"What?"

"You know."

Idiotic grin.

"It would be a good place to tap," he admitted.

HIS ROOM

or rooms, were in another forgotten subbasement, three levels above the forgotten basement we emerged from.

He slid back a steel door.

I expected his room to be lined with books.

It was lined with video monitors, computers, and radio scanners.

"Welcome to Shadow Pod central," he said.

Kate took off her shades and stared at the screens.

I recognized one of the screens.

It was the camera over the compound entrance.

People were coming and going.

They looked panicked.

"You've hacked into the Pod surveillance system," she said.

"Not all the cameras, but most of them. And the motion detectors. But what's been the most useful over the years are the radio communications. You kind of messed that up for me today when you tore that antenna out. I managed to fix it, but —"

"You fixed the antenna!" Kate said.

"How else was I going to monitor things? You probably know that Lod has tracking chips in those radios."

Kate nodded.

"I've hacked into those too. How do you think I knew you were coming to the reservoir all these years? I'm not a psychic."

"Or a ghost," I said.

"What?"

"Never mind," Kate said.

"Without the radios I wouldn't have known that the monster man and his dog were going to show up at the reservoir. He got down there just after me. I had to slip into one of my hidey-holes."

"Hidey-holes?" Kate said.

"I have 'em all over the place. And I always know where the closest one is in case I run into someone. How else could I survive down here all these years?"

Kate turned to me and smiled. "Poof," she said.

"Something like that. Anyway, when you put the radios on the dog, I knew you'd come to the reservoir. I still feel bad about that Rott but . . ."

He opened a drawer and pulled out two radios.

Kate grabbed them. "Enji is here?"

"Down the street. No dogs allowed in the library. They must have seen her run by with the radios on her collar but couldn't grab her."

"How did you catch her?" Coop asked.

"I had a friend pick her up when she got above, but we'll get to that in a minute."

He motioned us into another room, which turned out to be a kitchen.

Sitting on the table next to the oven were three well-used backpacks.

"Lod is going to come after you. You need to get out of the city tonight. I've put together a kit for each of you. Clothes, food, and toiletry items." He looked at me. "You can't return to your hotel. There are a couple of Shadows waiting there for you." He looked at Coop. "You can't go home and neither can Pat. Lod knows where you live. He knows everything about you."

He unzipped a side pocket and pulled out an iPhone.

"There's one for each of you, set up under bogus names, and you have unlimited everything on them. There are four numbers in the address book. Each other's" — he pulled an iPhone out of his back pocket — "and mine. Do not, and I mean *do not* under any circumstances call anyone else you've ever known, or any governmental organization, on these phones. Ever. That little room the Originals and Lod go into is filled with the most sophisticated computer equipment money can buy. In the old days he broke into buildings by picking locks and breaking windows. He does it electronically now, and he and the Originals are masters at this. If you call your home and talk to your parents from a landline, he'll have your number and know where you are in seconds. The same thing for their cell phones."

He looked at his watch.

"I'm going to have to hurry through the rest of this. When you get a chance you need to change your appearance.

Cut your hair . . . dye it. Maybe buy some fake eyeglasses. You can figure that out when you get someplace safe. My point is that all of you need to stay off the grid until I tell you that you're safe. Lod has people everywhere."

"Where should we go?" Coop asked.

"Newark Airport in Jersey shut down tonight because of weather. There are about five thousand angry holiday travelers stranded there. They aren't going to notice three more kids with backpacks. I want you to go there in separate taxis. Spend the night. In the morning get on a bus and go to the train station. You can't fly because you'll have to show ID, but you can always get on a train. When you're on the train, or bus, or however you're getting around . . . don't get on them together. Don't sit together. Don't talk to each other. Don't get off with each other. Lod's people are going to be looking for three kids. If you check into a hotel, pay cash, and don't check in together."

He looked at Coop.

"There's one stop I want you to make before you disappear."

"Where?"

"The FBI. I understand you have a friend there."

I looked at Coop, expecting him to say that he didn't have a friend in the FBI.

"I do," he said.

"Lod is up to something big and that means bad. You need to write down everything that's happened and give it to

238

her . . . but not personally. In each pack is a laptop. Put the information on a flash drive." He looked at me. "Do you still have that disposable cell phone you bought?"

"How'd you know I bought a cell phone?"

"Do you have it?"

"Yeah." The only way he could have known this is if he'd been following me up top.

"When you get to DC, Coop's going to make one call on it. Make it short. Then destroy the phone."

"Why don't we just call her right now?" Coop said. "We can put an end to this. They'll raid the Deep, find the mush rooms . . ."

The Librarian shook his head. "This isn't about growing mushrooms. And they aren't going to do anything on Christmas, or Sunday. Even your friend is in holiday mode. You need to talk to her when she's back at work. As soon as you do you need to get as far away from DC as you can. None of you will be safe until they have Lod and his people in custody. Even then you might not be safe."

"How did you know I knew someone in the FBI?"

"I know all about you. I've been checking into your background since the moment I met you. Belated happy birthday, by the way. And if I can find out that much about you, you can bet that Lod knows even more. I'm a rank amateur compared to him."

"Why did you check me out?"

The Librarian shrugged.

"A hunch," he said. "A strong feeling that you had something to do with this. That you were going to change everything. I can't explain it better than that. I don't understand it myself."

He looked at his watch again.

TIME TO GO

he said.

We picked up the packs and followed him out of the kitchen.

He slid the metal door open, looked up and down the hallway, then waved us through.

He locked the door behind us.

"Do you remember where you picked up the shopping carts last night?" he asked me.

"Yeah," I said. "It's just a few blocks from here. How do you —"

"Never mind," he interrupted. "My friend is waiting there." He looked at Kate and added, "With Enji. Get down there as quick as you can, then get over to Newark Airport."

"What about you?" Kate asked. "The mushroom man is going to tell Lod about what you did."

"I won't be the Librarian anymore," he said. "But I'll be fine. I have to button up some things here, then I'll be leaving town too."

We followed him down the hall to a stairway door.

He held it open for us, but Kate refused to go through.

"Who are you?" she asked. "Why have you been keeping track of the Pod all these years?"

He sat down on the bottom step and looked up at her as if he had known the question was coming but hoped it wouldn't.

"Because of you, Kate," he said quietly. "There were three bodies in that Dumpster. Not two. I was the third."

We waited.

"I was a member of the Pod. An Original. I went with Lod up top to find your parents. I had no idea he was planning to murder them. I tried to stop him. But it was dark that night . . . very dark. He shot me in the leg. But the second bullet intended for my head missed. It grazed my skull and knocked me out. He thought I was dead. I got out of the alley, with some help, and got to a hospital."

"Why didn't you call the police?"

"Because your parents were dead and I knew Lod wouldn't hurt you. If I called the police, you would have ended up in some kind of foster home. The Pod would have been destroyed. Back then I believed in what they were doing. And there were other problems . . ."

He looked up at Kate.

"My real name is Alex Dane."

His eyes teared.

"I'm your great-uncle. Lawrence Oliver Dane . . . Lod . . . is my older brother."

ALEX DANE

led us up the stairs to the front entrance of the library.

He keyed in the alarm code and opened the front door.

The sidewalks were covered in snow.

"Follow my instructions and you'll be okay. I'll call you when I can."

We stepped outside into the brisk air. I breathed in deeply.

"Merry Christmas," Alex said, and closed the door behind us.

No *friggin'* this time.

We walked down the street.

The only sound was our boots squeaking on the powdery snow.

We didn't make it to the storage locker.

The grocery cart came to us.

Pushed by Santa Claus.

Enji was sitting in the cart, shivering.

"So you're the girl," Santa said.

"Terry?" I said.

"Posty?" Coop said.

"Yeah."

He pulled his white beard down. Underneath was Terry Trueman, aka Posty, aka Saint Nick.

"Got tired of waiting for you, so I came looking. The Librarian gave us the heads-up about the Pod. We're spread out all over the city until this blows over. I thought the Santa suit would be a good disguise. And it's warm."

"What do you mean I'm the girl?" Kate asked.

"The girl whose parents were murdered."

"Oh. I guess I am that girl."

"Well, I'm the guy who found your parents in the alley. I also found the Librarian. Don't know his real name. Don't want to know his real name. When I called the police I left out a little detail. He had a bullet in his leg. It was clear that he had nothing to do with the murders. He showed up at the wrong Dumpster at the wrong time. That could have just as easily been me. I wanted to call an ambulance, but he begged me not to. He said he was in trouble with the police. I got him to an outpatient clinic where they don't ask a lot of questions . . . *then* I called the police."

He pulled a bag out of the cart.

"The Librarian told me that you and these two discovered that Lod killed your parents." He gave Kate the bag.

"What's in it?" Kate asked.

"Cash," Terry said. "The reward I posted after I found them. It's quadrupled since I put the money up." He looked at me. "I told you I was a pretty good banker."

"Thanks, Terry."

"No problem. I'm going to get off the street now and you better do the same."

The man in red turned the cart around and walked away.

FIVE

DAYLIGHT

DR. BERTRAND O'TOOLE

pulled up to the curb in front of his home in McLean in the back of a taxi.

He was alone, badly sunburned, peeling, bitten, and . . .

Bitter.

At the airport, Denise had jumped into a taxi by herself, saying that she would call him in a few days, and told him to give Vincent a peck on the beak for her, neglecting to peck Bertrand on the cheek good-bye. Glancing in the taxi's rearview mirror as he paid the fare, he could see why. His face was covered with inflamed red sores. He hoped none of them were nurturing insect larva.

"Jilted," he said under his breath.

"What's that?" the cabbie asked.

"Nothing," Bertrand said. "Keep the change."

He got out and yanked his heavy backpack from the trunk. The search for the elusive keel-billed motmot had been a complete disaster. It turned out that Denise was much better suited to the tropics than the Nobel laureate.

Bertrand did not think that Denise would be taking him on another expedition anytime soon, and that was fine with him. He'd had an absolutely miserable time.

He was lugging his mildewed pack up the walkway to his

front door when two burly men wearing FBI Windbreakers appeared out of nowhere.

"Mr. O'Toole?"

"*Dr.* O'Toole," Bertrand corrected.

"Fine, *Bert.* You need to come with us."

"Why? And my name is *Bertrand*, not Bert."

The agents smiled at his annoyance. They knew some things he didn't know they knew.

"It's a matter of national security."

"There must be some mistake. You obviously have the wrong O'Toole."

"No, sir."

"Can I put my things inside? Take a shower? Change clothes?"

"No, sir, you can't. And by standing out here we are compromising our operation."

"What operation?"

"You'll be fully briefed when you get to the WFO."

"WFO?"

"Washington Field Office."

"This is ridiculous. Do you know who I am?"

"Mr. Bert . . . sorry . . . Dr. Bertrand O'Toole, Nobel laureate, professor at Georgetown University, and you need to come with us . . . now."

The briefing actually started in the backseat of the agents' black SUV.

One of the agents passed Bertrand a document. The cover was stamped: CLASSIFIED. Below the red stamp were the words: BENEATH BY PAT AND COOP O'TOOLE.

DR. ARIEL O'TOOLE'S

holiday had not gone much better than her husband's.

The position at the Kennedy Space Center had fallen through at the last minute. (In fact, at the very moment her youngest son, Patrick, had pulled into Penn Station in New York City.)

In order to take her mind off losing the job, her boyfriend, Wayne, purchased a two-week Caribbean cruise for the *family* — five tickets at a ridiculously low fare. Because it was a last-minute deal they barely had time to pack and catch the ship before it sailed. The only person who knew where they were was their nanny, who took advantage of the unexpected time off by driving to California with her boyfriend.

Ariel actually loathed cruising but did not tell Wayne this. The only reason she had tolerated it when the boys were young was because of Patrick's claustrophobia. She was a lot more comfortable hurtling through the outer atmosphere than she was churning across the undulating sea.

She learned very quickly that sailing with Cooper and Patrick, as strange as they both were, was a breeze compared to cruising with three girls under the age of five without a nanny. It was like herding a troop of suicidal baboons on a dangerous island. When she wasn't changing dirty diapers and Pull-Ups, she was stopping the girls from jumping overboard. They climbed everything they could wrap their little fingers around.

Wayne was absolutely useless. He had spent the entire cruise trolling the ship for potential clients. After two weeks, Ariel was more exhausted than she'd been after her two-month stint aboard the International Space Station.

Her reaction to the two FBI agents waiting for her at the bottom of the gangplank was completely different than Bertrand's . . .

"Ariel O'Toole?"

"Yes."

"We're with the FBI."

"Good for you."

"We're here to escort you to the Washington Field Office in DC."

"What for?" Wayne asked.

"I'll go," Ariel said.

"What!" Wayne shouted.

Ariel handed Wayne his youngest daughter, hoping that when they arrived at the WFO they would lock her in a cell for a month by herself.

She fell asleep in the back of the black SUV on the way to the airport but perked up on the airplane when one of the agents passed her a document. The cover was stamped: CLASSIFIED. Below the red stamp were the words: BENEATH BY PAT AND COOP O'TOOLE.

THIS CAN'T BE TRUE

Bertrand said, holding up the document.

He and Ariel sat across the desk from Agent Ryan, whom they'd never thought they would see again.

"It's all true," Agent Ryan said.

"How do you know?" Ariel asked.

"As soon as I read it I led a team into the Deep."

Ariel and Bertrand both began to speak at the same time, but Agent Ryan held her hand up and cut them off.

"There's more to the document . . . a lot more. And it started before Coop inadvertently blew up your neighborhood."

"Cooper," Bertrand corrected.

Agent Ryan frowned. "I need you both to listen to me before you say anything else."

"Sorry," Bertrand said, surprising both Ariel and Agent Ryan.

Agent Ryan got up and started pacing as she talked.

BEFORE I MARRIED

before I joined the FBI, I was a cop in New York City.

"After we decided that Coop was just a kid digging a tunnel and not a terrorist, I had several conversations with him." Agent Ryan stopped pacing and looked at the O'Tooles. "Do you know why Coop dug that tunnel?"

"It was a lark," Bertrand said.

"Something to do," Ariel added.

"You didn't ask him, did you?"

"Not specifically," Ariel answered.

"I'm betting not at all," Agent Ryan said. "He said he was looking for something, but he didn't know what it was. Obviously not treasure. As you both know, Coop isn't interested in money. He told me that he had an overwhelming sense that he was destined to make an important discovery underground.

"Of course we had a team of psychologists examine him while he was here. They all came up with same verdict: perfectly sane."

Agent Ryan started pacing again.

"Coop and I got along well. I liked him. He stayed in touch with me. Once or twice a year he would drop by the WFO unannounced to check in with me. If I wasn't here, he'd leave a message saying that he had stopped by to see how I was doing. If I was here, he'd wait patiently until I had time to see him, and we'd talk."

"Was he still digging tunnels?" Ariel asked.

Agent Ryan shook her head. "He said he promised you he wouldn't. I don't think that means he wasn't doing some urban exploring underground, but he didn't take a shovel with him.

"In fact, he came by here on the day he argued with you two about his future. And for the record, I told him that he should go back home and go to college. I'm glad he didn't listen to me. But let's get back to what's not in the story Pat wrote down, because what's not there is even stranger than what is."

She took in a deep breath and let it out slowly.

"My maiden name is Muñoz. On Christmas Eve, nineteen years ago in New York City, I was the detective in charge of the man and the woman found shot to death in the Dumpster next to Pallotta's Italian Grill."

"Kate's parents?" Bertrand said.

"That's right."

"And you never told Cooper about this?" Ariel asked.

"I only discuss cases with other law enforcement officers. I don't even talk about them with my husband."

She took a flash drive and a cell phone out of her desk drawer.

"They dropped the flash drive in a trash can down the street next to the Ford's Theatre, along with the disposable cell phone they used to call me, and Pat's journal."

"When I started reading the document on the drive I thought it was a prank, even though that would have been so unlike Coop. But when I got to the part about Kate's parents I knew it was all true. There is no way any of them could have known about my involvement with that case. I had never talked to anyone about it, including other cops, because that case left a scar on me. All cops have one or two unsolved cases that they never get over. The so-called Dumpster Deaths case was mine. I knew it wasn't a random killing. I knew there was a child involved. But there were absolutely no leads. The blood trail stopped the moment Lawrence Oliver Dane walked out of the alley with Kate in his arms."

Agent Ryan looked out her window.

"You see," she continued, "the night they were murdered, everyone was staring at the sky. There wasn't a cloud from Ohio to New York. When Lawrence Dane shot his son and daughter-in-law, and his brother, we were all watching a lunar eclipse."

Agent Ryan turned back to the O'Tooles.

Both of their faces had paled.

Ariel took Bertrand's hand.

"Kate's parents were murdered around the time you were giving birth to Coop on the 495 Beltway in Virginia," Agent Ryan said. "Strange, isn't it?"

Stunned, Ariel and Bertrand nodded.

"I have no idea what it means. Or if it means anything. You're both scientists. What are the chances?"

"I'm an astrophysicist," Ariel said. "Not a metaphysicist, but I'll admit that it's a very strange coincidence."

"I'm a molecular biologist," Bertrand said, shaking his head, tightening his hold on Ariel's hand.

"Where are our sons?" Ariel asked.

"I'll let them speak for themselves in a moment. First, I want to tell you what we found in the Deep."

She opened a case folder marked: MR. LAWRENCE OLIVER DANE.

She showed them a mug shot of the man known as Lod.

Underneath the photo was a stamp that read: DECEASED.

OBVIOUSLY THAT'S NOT TRUE

Agent Ryan said.

"And he no longer looks like this. And he's not a mister, he's a doctor with PhDs in computer science, psychology, and dual master's degrees in business administration and agriculture. He attended UC Berkeley when he was fifteen, got his first undergraduate degree when he was seventeen. He's always liked nicknames. In his university days he was known as the Old Man . . . OLD being a play on his initials. He also liked staying under the radar. When we rounded up the Weathermen, we not only thought Dane was dead, we also thought he had been just a minor player. But it turns out that he was a big dog in the organization and happy to hide in the background. We reinterviewed the Weathermen who are still alive, and it seems that they had all conveniently forgotten to mention Dane and his involvement in the Weather Underground. They said they thought he was dead, and therefore unimportant, but I think some of them were lying. They knew he was still alive, and he's kept in touch with a select few over the years. It was clear from the interviews that they were afraid of him."

"Afraid," Bertrand said.

"Perhaps that's too mild," Agent Ryan corrected herself. "*Terrified* would be more accurate. We threatened his former conspirators with heavy jail time if they didn't tell us what they knew, but we were unable to turn any of them. Dr. Dane still has a hold on them. And I'm not sure if they are afraid that he'll kill them, or if he knows things about them they don't want us to know."

"Surely you have enough evidence to convict Dr. Dane of the murder of his son and daughter-in-law now," Bertrand said.

Agent Ryan shook her head and pointed at the document. "All we have is the word of a girl who alleges to be the victims' daughter. We would have to exhume their bodies. Run DNA on them, Kate, and her grandfather. Even if their DNA was a match it would be circumstantial evidence. There is nothing to connect Lawrence Dane to the alley on that night, except his brother, Alex, but he's long gone and I seriously doubt we'll find him until he wants us to. The good news is that we don't need any of that to convict Dr. Dane. We found enough in his compound to put him away for several lifetimes . . ."

On December 31, Agent Ryan led a task force of fifty people Beneath using a detailed map that Kate, Coop, and Pat had included on the flash drive.

THEIR FIRST STOP

was the Community.

It was abandoned.

There was a partially cooked turkey in the oven.

It took the task force several hours to reach the Deep.

It took them fifteen seconds to secure the area.

Seventy-nine people were arrested.

Sixteen dogs were captured.

Seven dogs got away.

Inside Lod's headquarters they found a secret room hidden behind a false bookcase. Inside the room was a bank of sophisticated computers. The hard disks had been wiped clean except for a single program called Fog. There was a digital timer ticking down on all the flat-screen monitors.

Second by second . . .

75:03 . . . 02 . . . 01 . . . 75:00 . . .

74:59 . . . 58 . . . 57 . . .

One hour and fifteen minutes to stop tens of thousands of people from dying.

The program was a fuse.

At zero it would release deadly sarin gas into Penn Station, Grand Central Terminal, several skyscrapers hosting New Year's celebrations, and the Deep.

They shut the program down with four minutes to spare.

As soon as it stopped another program booted up called Quake.

3:59 . . . 58 . . . 57 . . .

This program was the fuse for nearly forty pounds of C-4 explosives.

The plan was that after the Pod had been killed by the gas, Lod would bury them under several tons of debris.

"We stopped it with fifty-three seconds to go," Agent Ryan said.

"Cutting it kind of close," Bertrand said.

"The whole operation was too close," Agent Ryan said. "Coop and Pat put the flash drive in the trash can on the twenty-seventh. It took me three days to convince my superiors that this was a credible threat."

"Mass suicide," Ariel said quietly.

"Not quite mass, and certainly not suicide," Agent Ryan said. "Dr. Dane and the Originals were not in the Deep. According to those left behind they took off the day after Christmas to find his granddaughter, Kate. They expected them back any time. They knew nothing about his plan to gas and bury them."

"He got away?" Bertrand said.

"I'm afraid so."

Bertrand shook his head. "On the black market, sarin and C-4 would cost a fortune. How could a street person come up with that kind of money?"

"Larry Dane is no street person."

"Where did Dr. Dane get his money?" Ariel asked.

"Cloud's Mushrooms. The biggest supplier of mushrooms in the US. We have no idea how much money he made selling fungi over the years, but we believe it was tens of millions of dollars. The business was completely legitimate. The people running it above had never met the company's reclusive owner, and they didn't care. And they knew nothing about the mush rooms, two words.

"The blissfully ignorant corporate guys on top were making huge salaries. But that all ended Monday morning, December twenty-seventh. The company's cash was liquidated. It was transferred in rapid succession to different offshore accounts, then the money vanished altogether." Agent Ryan snapped her fingers. "Poof!"

"So he and his cohorts are on the loose with millions of dollars," Bertrand said.

"Right. When Kate and Coop and Pat got away, Lawrence knew it was all over for him. Kate and Alex were right. Lod was planning something big. Their escape moved the timetable up.

"And we have reason to believe the sarin gas and C-4 were just a prelude. He's been planning this for more than twenty years. The hornets are out of the nest, but we don't know where they are, where they're going, or who they're going to sting next. That's why we staked out both of your houses."

"My house too?" Ariel asked.

"And Wayne's," Agent Ryan added. "We've done a profile on Dr. Dane, and we believe that his brother is correct. He's looking for Kate and your sons. You and Bertrand are the only leads he has. You're both in grave danger. You'll be under twenty-four-hour surveillance until we apprehend Dr. Dane and his people."

"What about Cooper and Patr —" Bertrand stopped and glanced at Ariel. "*Coop* and *Pat*?"

Ariel smiled.

Agent Ryan did not smile. "I asked Coop to come in, but he refused. We're looking for them, but Kate is an expert at staying off the grid. And in a way, that is probably the safest place for them to be. Because Dr. Dane wiped his computers, we have no idea of the extent of his intel capabilities, but we think it's extensive. He's managed to obtain, or manufacture, sarin gas; procure military-grade C-4 explosives; and operate a multimillion-dollar business right under our noses without any of us knowing a thing about any of it."

"Do the kids know that Lod escaped?" Ariel asked.

"Not unless Alex told them." Agent Ryan took a digital tape recorder out of her pocket. "There was one other item with the flash drive . . . A memory stick. It was marked 'personal' and addressed to you two. Sorry, I listened to it. I'm a cop." She set the recorder on the desk. "I'll wait for you outside." She started out of her office, then stopped and looked at Bertrand. "Did you see a keel-billed motmot?"

"I did," Bertrand said. "But it wasn't worth it."

ARIEL AND BERTRAND

still holding hands, stared at the tape recorder, then looked at each other.

"What do you think?" Bertrand asked.

"Frightening and bizarre." Ariel paused, then added, "But Coop and Pat are heroes."

Bertrand nodded. "We underestimated them."

"Their whole lives," Ariel added. "I'm ashamed."

"I am too," Bertrand admitted.

"What happened to your face?"

"The tropical rain forest."

"How's Denise?"

"Unimpressed. How's Wayne?"

"Unhappy with my maternal instincts."

A few seconds of silence passed.

"I was thinking . . ." Bertrand began awkwardly. "I don't know what your situation is with —"

"I've missed you, Bertrand," Ariel said. "It would be easier for the FBI to keep an eye on us if we were together, and I really don't want to bring Wayne and his girls into all of this. It has nothing to do with them."

Tears welled up in Bertrand's eyes. "I've missed you too. Please come home."

Ariel smiled. "I will. I want to."

She picked up the recorder and slid the button to . . .

PLAY

If you're listening to this, it means Agent Ryan went garbage picking and found our package.

Hopefully she's acted on it.

If she hasn't, you need to convince her that everything on the flash drive is the absolute truth.

I know I'm a little quirky, as Pat says, but one of my quirks is that I don't lie, or exaggerate.

We don't know what Lod's up to, but I think it's going to hurt a lot of people.

He needs to be stopped.

As for us . . .

We're fine.

So far.

Pat and Kate are with me.

We'll lie low until we know we're safe.

If Alex knew everything about me, that means Lod knows everything too.

He also knows about you.

Lod is going to come looking for Kate.

It's too dangerous for Pat to come home right now.

Don't worry, I'll watch out for him.

Although it turns out that he was the one watching out for me. If it weren't for him, I'd be dead, or picking mushrooms in the dark.

And then there's Kate . . .

I think she's the reason I was driven Beneath.

Someday you'll meet her.

When you do you'll know why I had to look.

I was sorry to hear you two broke up.

I hope it's not permanent.

You make a good team.

You managed to keep us alive, which wasn't easy.

I know Pat wants to say something, but before I hand over the recorder I need to give you some warnings, which I hope don't freak you out too badly . . .

Kate is convinced that Lod had a contingency plan and put it into play as soon as we escaped.

She knows him better than anyone on earth.

I believe her.

Lod would not wait in the Deep for the FBI to show up.

He and the Originals have probably escaped.

We're proceeding as if he has.

Watch out for strangers hanging around the house or the university.

They might be Shadows.

Keep an eye out for stray dogs.

They might be Seekers.

Harden the security on your computers and phones, both at work and home. If you don't, Lod is going to hack into them.

Agent Ryan should be able to help you with this.

This last one is going to be hard for both of you . . .

You need to change your routines.

Daily.

Leave the house at different times.

Take different routes to wherever you're going.

Don't shop at the same grocery store.

Don't eat at the same restaurants.

Try not to let anyone know where you're going to be.

Basically . . .

You can't trust anyone.

If Lod can't hack into your personal information, he'll hack into someone's who knows you.

I'm so sorry to have put you into this terrible situation.

If something happens to either of you, I will never forgive myself.

Never.

Here's Pat . . .

Hi, Mom . . .

Hi, Dad . . .

There's not much I can add to what Coop just told you, except to say . . .

I love you.

I'm doing okay.

We'll be moving around until we know Lod and the Originals have been captured.

We're a little scared, but we are safe.

We are above . . .

ACKNOWLEDGMENTS

This book would not have been possible without my editor at Scholastic, Anamika Bhatnagar. You are the best! And a big thank-you is due to my wonderful agent, Barbara Kouts, and to the fabulous art director Phil Falco, who designs these books. Thanks also to Ellie Berger, David Levithan, Ed Masessa, Robin Hoffman, Lizette Serrano, Emily Heddleson, Antonio Gonzalez, Charisse Meloto, Saraciea Fennell, Elizabeth Starr Baer, Megan Bender, Adelle Pica, and everyone else in the Scholastic family. Big thanks to my good friends and first readers, Susan Stronach and Bob Jonas. But the biggest thanks, as always, goes to my wife, Marie, the kindest person in the room, every room, always.